Praise for
From the Windows of Diligence

"Each chapter of Jack Kohl's Circle of Fifths fable *From the Windows of Diligence* is a complex journey through the twelve major keys of the musical language. Mr. Kohl, who is an inveterate runner, composes a meditation; as thinker, runner, and musician, he revels in the hand position of each tonality. Mr. Kohl's prose is as dense as the forest he trods. It is nothing less than a tour de force. The prose is sparse, erudite, nostalgic, lyric; one smells the earth, feels the crackle of leaves. There is the singular faith of the solitary wanderer; ears, eyes, and body wide open with wonder. *The Windows of Diligence* is life-affirming, and I believe it will become a classic as is *Walden*."

—David Dubal, Author of *The Essential Canon*
of Classical Music

"In this second volume of essays, pianist and writer Jack Kohl takes the Makamah Trail in New York State as a physical and philosophical roadmap for a series of thoughtful and erudite ponderings which meld the craft and philosophy of the piano and those who play it with reminiscences on childhood, travel, people and nature."

—Frances Wilson, pianist and writer;
"The Cross-Eyed Pianist"

"Is this a book about running seen through the lens of music, or about music seen through the lens of running? Jack Kohl's engaging propensity for taking life as a metaphor for music (rather than the more intuitive other way around) stands things on their heads, and makes you look at your environment differently. His as-outdoors-so-indoors mysticism turns hills into black piano keys, untuned pianos into forests, and practice-room denizens into deer in their habitat. It's a reminder that our perceptions can be richer and livelier than our habits let them be."

—Kyle Gann, author of *Charles Ives's Concord: Essays after a Sonata*

"Thoreau took us on a leisurely boat ride and gave us *A Week on the Concord and Merrimack Rivers*, replete with philosophical musings as well as detailed natural history. Here we accompany Jack Kohl on a series of jogs through Long Island's Makamah Preserve as he organizes his observations around the "Circle of Fifths," the twelve tones of the chromatic scale. The result is witty, wry, and replete with the wisdom gained from his close attention to nature and a lifelong devotion to music, to which two other, complementary, essays typify."

—Philip F. Gura, Author of *American Transcendentalism: A History*

"Hooray, another book from Jack Kohl! In *From the Windows of Diligence*, we are once again treated to Jack's unique ability to fuse his two great passions, trail running and musical composition and structure. And once again, we are not disappointed. Jack bestows his insights and lyrical gifts, sentence after sentence, paragraph after paragraph, page after page. This tightly composed collection of essays, following Jack's daily circular trail run as musical theorist's Circle of Fifths, is full of surprise and delight, whimsy, and laugh-out-loud humor. We're lucky to have Jack's writing to remind us of the small daily miracles everywhere, both around and within all of us."

—Gordon Bakoulis, five-time U.S. Olympic marathon trials qualifier, editorial director of New York Road Runners

"Only a writer of Jack Kohl's intellect and imagination could interweave such a rich meditation on nature, running and music, and make it all hang together. Kohl goes deep but never loses his sense of purpose nor his sense of humor. Who else could see the runner and the circle of fifths as the action of a giant piano hand? Reading him makes you want to know him."

—Michael Johnson, essayist, critic, and portrait artist whose work has appeared in the New York Times International, FactsandArts.com, Boston Musical Intelligencer, among others

OTHER TITLES BY JACK KOHL

Essays:

Bone Over Ivory

The Pauktaug Trilogy:

That Iron String

Loco-Motive

You, Knighted States

Available in print and ebook at Amazon.com
and other online booksellers

From the
WINDOWS
of
DILIGENCE

Essays from a Standing Pianist

JACK KOHL

THE PAUKTAUG PRESS

Pauktaug, New York

Published by:
The Pauktaug Press
Pauktaug, New York

Copyright © 2021 by Jack Kohl

ISBN: 978-0-578-79152-4

Cover illustration and map:
Freiman Stoltzfus • www.freimanstoltzfus.com

Interior design:
Gary A. Rosenberg • www.thebookcouple.com

Printed in the United States of America

Contents

Foreword by Jeffrey M. Duban   ix

Makamah and the Circle of Fifths   1

D-flat (7 o'clock): The Christmas Tree   9

A-flat (8 o'clock): Valley of the Oaks   12

E-flat (9 o'clock):
Beautiful-Girl-and-Two-Dogs-and-Turtle   16

B-flat (10 o'clock): The Dead Goose   27

F-Major (11 o'clock): The Ruin   32

C-major (12 o'clock): Wetlands Overlook   47

G-major (1 o'clock): The Dead Raccoon   52

D-major (2 o'clock): Deer Curve   62

A-major (3 o'clock): Steve of Makamah   68

E-major (4 o'clock): Tree Carvings   75

B-Major (5 o'clock): Arrowhead Creek   81

G-flat: Tattoo Girl and the Erratic   85

Conclusion   91

Backphrasing: Musical Theater and the Newtonian Clock   95

Practice Rooms: From the Windows of Diligence   115

About the Author   141

Foreword

In both this and his first collection of essays, *Bone Over Ivory*, author Jack Kohl reveals the esthetician and synesthetician within, wringing from the minute, fleeting, or imperceptible a universal if not cosmic cohesion. Indeed, Kohl's insights recall those of Emerson, Thoreau, Eiseley, and even Proust, Kohl himself a Transcendentalist to the core (see his magisterial "A Transcendentalist's Love Story" from *Bone Over Ivory*). A lifelong pianist, Kohl holds forth within the context of the Circle of Fifths, defined as the relationship between the twelve tones of the chromatic scale, their corresponding key signatures, and associated major and minor keys. The new essays thus present a "music of the spheres" modulated, if you will, to a terrestrial setting, as Kohl ever fixes on his immediate physical surroundings. In the process, he invokes musical keys to give personally important places more importance yet, effectively playing geographical and musical intervals off against each other.

Kohl's special place is Northport Village (Long Island) and environs (where he grew up and lives to this day)—Fort Solonga Road, Makamah Preserve, Sunken Meadow State Park, Tiffany Creek Preserve of Oyster Bay—all descriptively recessed and glinting forth as so many Sisley landscapes en plein air (see e.g., Sisley, "Street Entering the Village," 1880). As Lawrence Durrell has observed, "We are children of our landscape, it dictates behavior and even thought in the measure to which we are responsive to it" (*Justine*). Kohl's beloved Northport and its reverberant surroundings thus hover over these essays as pedaled piano notes. One may compare the evocation of Combray, the imagined village of Proust's childhood. Kohl is landscape-soldered, secure in his setting, including the running paths with which he communes. Indeed, the shared demands and rewards—and required stamina—of running and piano-playing are integral to Kohl's synthesis.

The reader will marvel, for instance, at Kohl's conjured "figurative practice room of the forest," his "movement from manual hands, to the one, imagined, comprehensive hand (to the Runner as Giant Piano Hand)," and, to be sure, "the beautiful woman of E-flat," i.e., the amnesia-inducing "beautiful, fit, women in running tights and yoga pants. . . stand[ing] in wild analogy to many black, grand pianos. . . . go[ne] suggestively out of tune in secret." Of all the instruments, the pear-shaped cello is most suggestive of a woman's curvature and form—and the cellist's embrace of the instrument most similar, in its intimacy, to human embrace. That Kohl sees it differently is one of the many wonderfully unexpected provocations of these essays.

—Jeffrey M. Duban, author, *The Lesbian Lyre and The Shipwreck Sea*

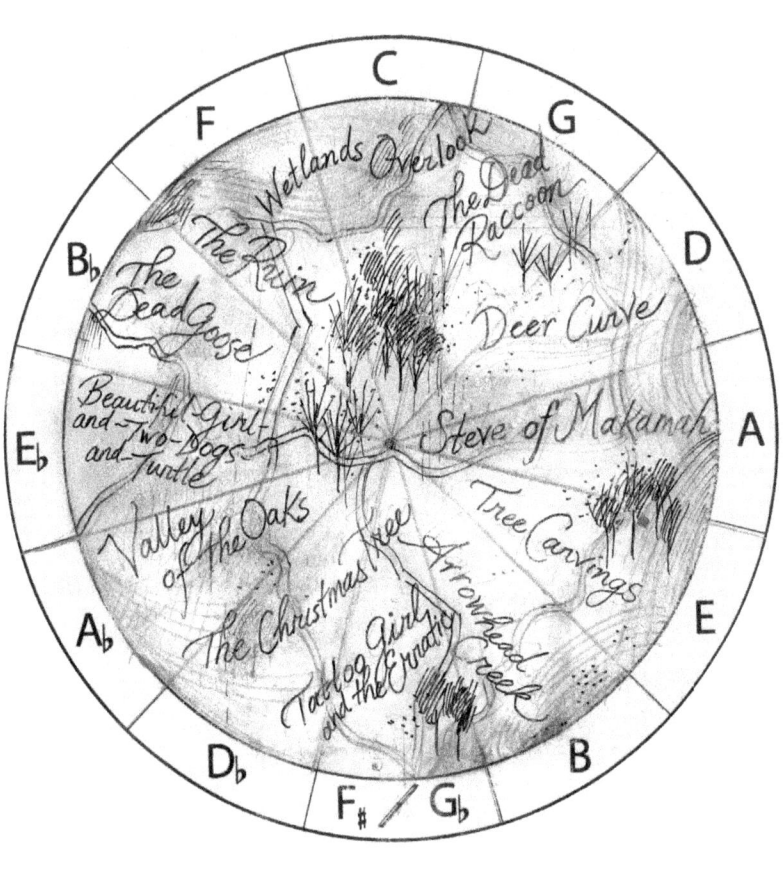

Makamah and the Circle of Fifths

Nearly to the time of my third birthday I lived in a garden apartment in Flushing, Queens. There I rode my wooden ride-on tractor. I submit that the tractor was as my first introduction to sitting at a piano, and propelling it by pushing with one's feet along the ground was as my first idea of working the piano's pedals from a seated position. The tractor's small, front, double-wheel even suggested the heavy double-casters on the legs of many concert grands. When I made my endless loops in the garden apartment courtyard did I show a tendency to follow a clockwise or counterclockwise course? What deep instincts or deliberation influenced the selection? I have asked my mother and father if they recall my common choice of direction. My mother was certain it was counterclockwise. My father thought it was clockwise;

when I asked him again he said counterclockwise. I am uncertain for myself.

From Queens my mother and father and I moved to Northport Village. Perhaps my earliest memory of the Long Island town in which I still live is of the hilltop just outside of the office of the contractor who built my family's home. Sometime before or during the construction, in 1972 or early 1973—about halfway to late in my second year of life—we visited that office, located in a house that still stands today on the south side of Fort Salonga Road (Route 25A), on a site called Pebble Hill, just to the east of Northport Village. Unknown to me at that time was a forest preserve of about 140 acres, one hundred yards or so east from Pebble Hill and on the north side of the road. The preserve was originally called Crab Meadow Park East Watershed. In 1973, almost at the same time of my visit to Pebble Hill, the forest nearby was renamed Makamah Preserve. I wish I had been taken there on that day of my first memory of Pebble Hill, and that I would have retained then an impression of how that forest looked nearly fifty years ago.

On the day of that visit to Pebble Hill we may

have gone next to the scene that competes for my earliest memory of Long Island: to the building site of my family's home in Northport Village. I can still see my father in my mind—wearing a Sasquatch-brown coat—standing at a distance in the midst of the house's mere frame as I waited in the car with my mother. I know now where pianos were to stand in later years amidst those then exposed vertical posts, the studs looking like straight and tall old oaks to my short self.

There are now times in my life when I run in Makamah almost every day. On countless afternoons I have traded the practice room for a drive to the forest's parking lot on Fort Salonga Road. The preserve has a third-of-a-mile yellow-blazed access trail from the road, leading to a 1.6-mile white-blazed circular trail: a looped courtyard in the trees. The parking lot sometimes reveals if there are other occupants inside the figurative practice room of the forest, for such a practice room is one that can be shared. The rear bumpers of cars in the lot often suggest the nature of other users' practicing: Ironman Watch decals, stickers that boast 13.1 or 26.2, or empty mountain bike racks. However, one does not always encounter the other users.

The trailhead sign even resembles a ruinous schedule placard adjacent to a practice room door. But unlike such a neglected signup sheet in a music school—worn by vandalism—the trailhead sign demonstrates its principal wear from the elements. Often the maps and postings on the latter are rendered unreadable by the sun and rain. I have seen the lettering decals on some trail signs curled up to such an extent by weathering, that the words resemble the most ancient carvings of initials in the roughest bark.

Sometimes the lot is empty when I arrive because of the weather. I often seek out the figurative practice room of the forest most at such times, as much because there is likely to be less competition during rain and snow as because of the beauty of the putative inclemency. I am often disappointed when a forecast of storms seems like it may remain unrealized. "Hopefully conditions will have deteriorated by the time I reach the trail," I remark to myself.

On snowy days in the empty lot, abandoned walking sticks lean against the trailhead sign or the adjacent trees. But one may still note inbound footprints of a predecessor at the start of the yellow-blazed access trail, sometimes one to two hours old if the snow is light.

When I enter the yellow-blazed and ascending access trail, it is as if I am walking into a practice room with an elongated vestibule that precedes the main workspace. I move as if into a practice room as one who prepares to rehearse musical abstractions rather than finished pieces: abstractions such as scales in all twelve keys around the Circle of Fifths—as if expecting from the run no art but principally a circuit of tactile routine. I resist offering a definition here of the Circle of Fifths. Almost any reference work can provide a sound answer. I also submit that any layman put aside misgivings to technical allusions I may make from the musician's trade. For as Richard Henry Dana observes in the Preface to his *Two Years Before the Mast*, many readers can "follow the minute nautical manœuvres . . . who do not know the name of a rope in the ship. . . ."

The yellow-blazed access trail, though undulating, is principally one of steep ascent, leading not only to the intersection with Makamah's white-blazed loop trail, but to the forest's point of highest elevation, just before the intersection. When I stand on that highest point of the yellow-blazed access trail and look down to the highest point of the white-blazed trail just below, I measure a distance as that of the pianist's between his eyes and his hands.

Why should Makamah's white-blazed loop suggest so much to me the G-flat (the six o'clock) position on the Circle of Fifths when I join it at this intersection? Again, the circuit here is at its highest elevation, and at the G-flat position on the Circle of Fifths one encounters a scale not only with all five black keys of the keyboard employed, but with three of those elevating black keys encountered right away by the fingers. G-flat presents the hand with the most concentrated and immediate sense of altitude in a scale.

Does this suggest that a black-key-less C-major must await me at the farthest position in the outbound descent of the run, at the twelve-o'clock position of the forest's figurative Circle of Fifths? Yes, it does. For the trail at last parallels a wetland, flooded at high tide and parallel with sea level, the lowest point one can find on my native island.

Makamah's white-blazed trail is a circuit, but it is not a perfect circle. Yet when I join any loop that I run with frequency, the critical question of direction remains a preoccupation. And why do I sometimes feel regret in the choice I make, or hold a sense of ambivalence about the decision over the course of the run, even though I am sure to cover all the ground no matter which direction I choose at the intersection? A sense of importance in the option is with me even in the dark when I reach the intersection at night.

Permit me now, in this instance, to turn left at the intersection. I will share the names and associations that have come to me at key points along the circuit when traveling clockwise. In other forests I have noted mountain bike trails that present signs with names for the sections of the looped trails. Such trails ask that riding traffic always flow in a clockwise direction. When a runner travels such trails in reverse, the little signs with the section names present their blank sides, and the names remain a mystery. I have posted no signs myself in Makamah. I share the names only with you.

This run commences with the pianist's concentration moving from manual hands to the one, imagined, comprehensive hand (to the Runner as Giant Piano Hand)—with the head standing in analogy to the miraculous thumb (for it is the thumb, at last, that makes all the best connections), and the legs serving in analogy to fingers two and three of an idealized right hand, and the arms as four and five. But, at last, those analogies may shift as one plays to strengths in an uneven trail run.

All I have given thus far and will continue to relate is taken from journal pages in most cases spaced apart by considerable amounts of time— great spaces between utterances of the unbidden truth, and one may then suspect that the result is as a work of fable. But do we not blink even in the midst of an unremitting stare, in the midst of unrelenting focus on a sequential actuality? I may have blinked while assembling this essay, but never as much as one who cries or who has something in the eye, and much less than one who naps or sleeps! And does not one who blinks infrequently unnerve us? Such an eye is tantamount to the unblinking of the dead.

D-flat (7 o'clock): The Christmas Tree

As one joins the white-blazed circuit and leaves behind G-flat—and begins the slow descent of the loop's first half—D-flat's section soon appears. D-flat still has all five black keys in its scale as played upon the keyboard.

Standing on the right of the trail, recessed in the midst of other trees, appears a premonitory symbol at the start of one's circuit. There one can see a Christmas tree—not a Christmas tree by usual species, for it is a large holly, but a tree adorned with painted glass Christmas balls. These ornaments have stood in place for years. Perhaps they are kept in place by the original decorator. I note that almost no trail system or preserve on Long Island is without such a Christmas tree. I know of two on the Meadowlark Mountain Bike Trail, one in Sunken Meadow State Park, one in Tiffany Creek Preserve of Oyster Bay, and two in the West Hills of Huntington (one of the latter two on Jaynes Hill, making it perhaps the highest Christmas tree on Long Island). Ornaments on such trees take on a weathered and bleached appearance very quickly.

It seems that people who sentence ornaments to these trees are accelerating the eradication of some burdensome memory. The distorted reflections that such ornaments present make me think of the colonies of wild parakeets that can be found on Long Island. I have heard tell of one colony in a large evergreen tree in Valley Stream; another is reputed to be in Babylon. Their nests are said to be enormous. If a trail's Christmas tree had such a colony, might one hear an echo of one's voice from within it, as distorted as one's reflection from the glass ornaments?

Seeing the Christmas tree so early on a clockwise circuit of Makamah reminds me of that preluding force of Christmas day's approach to a little boy (a power I would have suspended as a Perpetual Preluding), an approach so strong throughout my early life that I can recall the degree of sentimental agony with which (on Christmas Day) I could no longer identify with songs with which I had complete identification only the day before (on Christmas Eve). The words of those songs are so deeply connected with Preluding: "It's *Beginning* to look a lot like Christmas" and "*Soon* it will be Christmas Day" and "'Twas the night *before* Christmas"—all connected with a state of anticipation one wishes to freeze. The songs and the scenes in their music box snow globes seemed privileged to remain in their glorious Perpetual Preluding of Christmas Eve whilst I had been forced to advance to Christmas Day! In recent years—and only in recent years, really—a temperance to this pain has come about due to a perception of seemingly accelerating time with advancement of personal age. For it is now easy to think of Christmas as prospective again as soon as it has arrived or just passed. But what a price to pay for that alleviation, for mortality waits near the ultimate realization when each succeeding Christmas is flush against its predecessor. Yet is that sense of accelerating time at last a benign thing—a premonition of an unticking eternity, a Cosmos floated on a Perpetual Prelude, on an endless Eve, even to all who reach their personal mortality?

For now I content myself in the search for parakeets in the Christmas trees of the trails, where the Eve of me is stored in an echo.

A-flat (8 o'clock): Valley of the Oaks

A-flat is an area with lovely, maturing, almost mighty oaks, none of which at the same time obscures the distant prospect afforded by the grand and descending slope. I call this area a Valley of Oaks. I never begin this descent but that I think of the music theory discipline of Schenkerian analysis, a method that invokes examination at a foreground, middleground, and, at last, universally distilled background level. The close trees (the foreground) pass with one's rate of running, the middleground trees more slowly, and the most distant trees almost not at all. I mutter to myself when I begin this descent, "I see Schenker in the oaks."

Though A-flat has lost a black key, and the Runner as Giant Piano Hand feels the first real descent into the circuit on reaching this position, there remains a sense of Preluding. It was indeed on a recent Thanksgiving Eve—and this on a night before a full moon—that I had at A-flat a most remarkable adventure of approaches. Early in my descent into the cold Valley of the Oaks, in the eleventh hour of the night, I heard Canadian Geese passing overhead in formation.

Did I first notice the great cloud-shadow effect crawling on the ground and then credit it by looking above to the moon and the clouds? Or had I looked up first to see the clouds taking the moon and then looked down to see the result? Perhaps it was the latter, precipitated by the trumpet cue of the passing geese. I saw a frontier of blue moonlight coming toward me up the dark slope of the Valley of Oaks, the shadow before it being pulled away. So much of life attributes to us our actual or figurative exchange of lenses for the register of change in fixed perspectives. But there I paused in my run, stood solid, as much my unchanged self as I was in the moments before, when it came time to witness the great rolling of the forest from shadow-black to brilliant blue. I was in the company of my trusted running friend, Mr. Peter Klann, on this night, and I heard us both mutter in perfect concert at this instant, "Here it comes!"

As I looked down the long slope of the Valley of Oaks, the trees showed—from bases to canopies—the advance of this blue wall of moonlight. But I could also mark the approach of the blue frontier along the ground. Its cloud-blown pace challenged some part of the fearful self to see if it could be outrun. One can make oneself giddy in the summer surf with the game of trying to escape the inescapable by running landward from a wave—intentionally inducing, then, a happy fear. The approach of this blue wall recalled that feeling for me, but supernaturally intensified. I felt, perhaps, I should duck or turn from it while knowing no bodily sensation could come from its wave. But, still, I felt the impulse to react. I did not react, at last, yet I felt the strike of this wave when it hit me though I felt it not. 'Twas as to stand on ground and watch Impersonalized Deity toy with gerrymandering borders as a Personalized God.

The moonlight of this wave was as if one had the privilege to remain for a time in the ambient shine from a strike of lighting. I know that for some electronic devices, pausing them for too long is said to threaten damage to their screens. The intensity of the moonlight on this night gave one the impression that some Providential mechanism had been strained to permit such a privileged pause. Was the screen of God's revelation overburdened by this night? Is the obligation of testifying to that moment of paused Creation the duty of anyone who was permitted to see it? I feel compelled to give a report of when God blinked slowly. Is it fortunate that there is not an analogous means of wandering in an elongated utterance of a thunderclap, as well? But if there was—and one could manage the titan-fortissimo of that fermata—would it not be like rendering the forest into the grandest piano, one with which the thinking student could pause over any note interminably, without fear of the sound's instant decay?

This idea has always haunted me: Though I have lived near the places of which I write for all of my life, when the earliest distant and solitary rumble of spring thunder arrives, and when, in close complement, the first rogue and remote fireworks are detonated in early summer, I lose certainty of the landscape between myself and the source of those sounds. With such booms comes a flash of new insight into ostensibly known areas, a hint of interiors that cannot fit into my former surveys of the actual terrain. With such sounds the count of acres in a finite square appears to go up. This never fails. It always happens, no matter how expert I become about Northport's and Makamah's geography. It often happens that I place the real but not actual new count of acres in the midst of forest areas. But this is not always so, for I sense this expansion even in the strict lots of the village.

E-flat (9 o'clock): Beautiful-Girl-and-Two-Dogs-and-Turtle

Though there is a net downhill in this journey along the first half of Makamah's circle, there are ups and downs along the way. As one engages with practicing scales in each of the keys in a journey around an actual Circle of Fifths, undulation is also inevitable. For all keys but one (C-major) are collections of black and white keys. How, then, is a constant sense of metaphorical descent registered for he who thinks as a Runner as Giant Piano Hand? Again, the journey on this woodland Circle of Fifths appears to start from G-flat because of the suggestiveness of the white-blazed trail beginning at the highest point on the circuit—and this earthly elevation in analogy to the elevation of the fingers in a scale with all five black keys employed—but also because a clockwise journey on the Circle of 5ths from G-flat traces an earlier and earlier engagement and agency of the thumb (the head of the Runner as Giant Piano Hand), almost with the motion to each new key. With the G-flat scale the thumb enters on the fourth degree; with D-flat and A-flat it enters on the third; but with the key of E-flat and its successor (B-flat) the thumb enters as early as the second degree in the ascending scale! Soon the thumb, the head, will be engaged before all!

It was along one of the somewhat superficial but noticeable rises in the trail, and just before its descent to E-flat's most definitive position, that I first meditated the initials carved into the bark of one of Makamah's trees (dated 1973, in coincidence with my earliest memories of Northport). But not far past this carving I once met a figure who, had I known her name, would have given me cause to leave her initials in bark next to mine.

On a rainy afternoon in early July, again in the company of Mr. Klann—for sometimes one enters practice rooms with others, and it is then that practicing is thought of as *rehearsal*—I came upon an Eastern Box Turtle on this section of the trail.

When I encounter Box Turtles on my adventures, I always find them *on* the trail; I do not see them *from* the trail. Does the rain drive them onto the path? Does the circuit offer them, as for me, easy motion offered by its cleared plane? I never need to step aside for turtles on the trail; I just step over them.

I came upon this turtle (it had yellow markings on its shell) right at the white circuit's intersection with another, shorter, trail that offers an exit from the loop. This spot has become E-flat for me on Makamah's Circle of 5ths. I call it the intersection of Beautiful-Girl-And-Two-Dogs-And-Turtle. New experience in the New World woods mimics the creation of place names from American Indian lore, though the lore is one's own.

I preceded my running friend by a few yards as I came upon this intersection. But before I could remark for very long on the turtle in the rain, Mr. Klann muttered, "Look what we have here!" A beautiful young woman approached. She had long, dark, straight hair and olive skin and wore taut black yoga pants. She appeared from a side trail that is marked with faded yellow blazes formed into the pattern of a bear's paw. As if in living complement of the paw blazes, the young woman was preceded by two dogs.

Beautiful, fit, women in running tights and yoga pants, seen in the woods, stand for me in wild analogy to many polished, black, grand pianos. One can find these perfect, dusted, yet untuned pianos in countless affluent homes. These pianos go suggestively out of tune in secret; they grow wild unnoticed and would seem, at first, the last object to have more in common with the forest than the living room. As one need do with such pianos to learn the truth, one must at last kiss the beautiful young women in running tights, or make real visceral contact or have intercourse with them, to see if they are out of tune with the parlor and in tune with the shifting forest. Like a curved and neglected black Steinway, beautiful young women in tight yoga pants are so smoothed, so externally idealized, that they can give amnesia to the worldly man—for the tights often give the impression that feminine genitalia are level with the body's other adjacent surfaces. Running tights and yoga pants about the midsection of a young woman make one think of classical statues that do not depict the sclera or pupil; they restore a hope even in the lustful and rakish man that female genitalia are as a classical statue's eye, represented for its function, but rendered as smooth as a C-major scale. The sanded curves and sheen of a grand piano sublimate the textured interior of its mechanics, as well.

In my worldly searches I have noted that the yoga pants and tights worn by beautiful women have text written often on the rear, the static words animated by the motion of young ladies' buttocks. This writing is in analogy to a piano company's label on a seductively open fallboard, and this analogy perhaps purifies my initially prurient tendency to gravitate to any gym's second row of treadmills.

Man gains something when he lets the great pianos of the parlors go out of tune; he also glimpses a raw grace from the impression given by the seductively curved, usually closed and textless fallboard and lid of the young woman in the forest. But one must eventually tune the piano in the parlor, and one cannot ask a beautiful female stranger to disrobe on the trail. Yet meeting the woman at E-flat suggests finding a perfectly glossy grand that has been abandoned to the woods, one that may go out of tune without interference, its lid left open to the rain. However, this woman of E-flat is still not the ultimate goddess-beast for whom I yet search.

I have been looking for a long time. I recall with fascination that in kindergarten I looked across a table to my chum Josh's drawing of his family. The forms were rendered as heads and legs without torsos. Grand pianos in actuality do not look unlike young Josh's depictions of purified people; grand pianos appear as all legs and heads to me at times. They go so far as to suggest that they have no reproducing organs at all.

And I should note that if I were to find on the trail, instead of the goddess-beast, the fabled abandoned piano to which I allude above, it would be a very different creature than the one that now sits silent in the chamber of the once-driven player who no longer possesses drive—or who, better said, has conquered his drive or redirected it. There is a great difference between the neglected piano of idle luxury and the abandoned piano of some disaffected pianists.

The latter kind of piano has surely created pianists who yearn to leave the instrument, has fostered King Midas players who wish their cultivated hands to go out of practice for fear that otherwise all they touch will, at last, turn to sound and then depend upon the player for its longevity. I have noted that when I am too much in practice as a pianist when I run, it is as if focus is drawn away from the forest's trail and kept in my hands. Impulses in my hands cue thoughts of the remembered practicing. My hands can then ruin the run, and not because I fear for them in a fall.

Such disaffected pianists tire of mediating the speed and force of their digital attack even upon indifferent objects, lest those objects become mortal notes—they due, moments after being struck to life, to decay immediately. After applying a Midas Touch, a sense of paternity causes such a pianist to hold any figurative note he has struck, to preserve as long as possible any object he has brought to life, before the dampers come down. Do not certain pianists walk about thinking that one can raise the dampers behind all objects for a time? Who among pianists has not sat in a midnight practice room, holding on to a single note or chord with the hand or the depressed damper pedal until the sonority dies away and is indistinguishable from the ringing in one's ears or the buzz of light bulbs above? How many things do I touch and then fear

I have a responsibility for the life of a tone created by the contact? What figurative pitch do I produce when I press the button that summons an elevator? What dampers do I keep raised, as if in squeezing another's hand in a romance, one that will slip away if I let go? There is nothing quite like the damper that hovers over nearly each string on a piano—nothing quite like it on any other instrument. Some instruments have a chance of perpetuating a sound after a player steps away, but a piano is actively muted by its mechanism as soon as the hand is raised from the key. When I have sat at a musical theater rehearsal piano, I have noted the conflated and captured sound of a cast's voices when I have ridden the damper pedal in silence as they shouted—their scattered voices captured into that concentrated place, that trap like the smooth and flat Phantom Zone of Superman lore. I hold onto the cast's lives of five seconds preceding the present with my depressed right foot.

There are no macabre, independent, ventriloquist dummies in the census of pianos; the hand or foot must be on the doll for it to speak. But some players are trying to stand farther and farther from the doll. Note the twentieth-century trend of standing before an open grand's side and reaching in to play directly on its strings. Thus the course of the piano's history has the player walking away from the keyboard and bench, but still playing the instrument– yet soon to be so far that the keyboard may be miles away and the fallboard closed during a concert, the ebony reached from the distance of living oaks.

Like the pianist who passes from piano to piano on a late and empty night in a conservatory's or university's practice area, the disaffected pianist is as the single candle being passed from new jack-o-lantern to new jack-o-lantern on the night of carving to test the faces. The disaffected pianist as candle wanders, at last, from this October to the forests of out-of-tune November in search of the goddess-beast. It is when the squirrels come to offer mad plastic surgery to the jack-o-lanterns of November, on the nights when the surviving faces of cut pumpkins are sunken, and sinking in further still like that of an old-time gummer, that the lanterns seem most to have earned their right to Midas Candle glow. Since I always pull up a bench and linger about the faces at the end of Hallow-een night, and hesitate for the longest moments to blow them finally out, perhaps I am not lamenting that a year must pass before their kind may reappear, but fear that I will not have the resolution to search and give them their just due in November.

The disaffected pianist is as the large jack-o-lantern candle that sometimes lasts to another year. When one finds such a survivor, does the melted wax memorialize the pattern of how the departed face admitted the wind? I look for immortalized triangles and grins. Then, in grayest December, I sometimes find the bases of the largest candles in the snow. The squirrels cannot eat the soul. I pick up these fragments and wonder at them, for they are like finding ticket stubs in an old coat.

There is, at last, no escape for this Midas, this particular Jack of the lantern. I have never practiced the piano harder than when I have been running in the woods. Nearly all pianists leave the practice room and go out to perform, and thus hide themselves and shun a greater labor. But I have never practiced the piano harder than when I do not practice and do not play—and now work many hours for every single hour of my practicing past so as to harvest the old implications. Or is this little book just the most industrious effort of the laziest musician?

Or have I made a career from studying the realization that I had prepared for the wrong one?

I thought such things as I stared in astonishment at the sight of the beautiful woman of E-flat. I exclaimed to her (as if acknowledging our mutual attraction to the woods under rain), "You have the same idea!" I asked after the names of the two dogs, yet I cannot recall them now. One of the dogs investigated the turtle. The young woman expressed concern for the turtle. But Mr. Klann assured her that the dog would learn quickly if snipped by the turtle's little jaws.

We parted from the young woman, and I said, "Be careful out here!" When we were out of range of Beautiful-Girl-And-Two-Dogs-And-Turtle, I extolled the woman's beauty to my companion. We did not see her or her dogs again. However, when I return almost each day to this E-flat position on the circuit, I think first of that turtle, he the smallest of all the characters of the incident. Yet he stood fast at that spot after all others had left.

B-flat (10 o'clock): The Dead Goose

B-flat is not far from E-flat on Makamah's Circle of Fifths, yet it distinguishes itself quickly from its predecessor. Just past another small climb and descent, in a valley just before the woods of B-flat rise to a startling view of the adjacent Crab Meadow Golf Course, on an April twenty-seventh afternoon I came across the eviscerated body of a Canadian Goose on its back. It lay right in the center of the trail. Along with disembowelment, it had neither legs, nor neck, nor head. Neither viscera nor stray feathers rested near the body or the site. Was the goose a victim of a hawk or eagle or fox? Often in my journal I will mention an incident when I come across the *body* of a dead bird, but this is a case where the word *carcass* may be more fitting. This body had the visible heft of a carcass, though even the smallest bird's body found on the trail will, before seen, betray itself by a scent comparable to that of a much larger animal's carcass. When I come across the bodies of small birds after first catching their scent as carrion, I am often surprised that some other presence has not carried off the prize before my clumsy arrival. Yet I had not caught the scent of this goose carcass before I saw it. Two days later, on April twenty-ninth, when I came to the same spot, I neither smelled nor saw the carcass. It was gone. But on ascending the slope beyond the little dip in which I had seen the dead goose, I saw at last some evidence of white, downy, feathers. Perhaps I had not dreamed the goose murder!

Crab Meadow Golf course came into view. The golf course's fence conjured a poor comparison with the wall of the cloud-shadow effect of A-flat. I had felt a fear of the latter's intangibility, had felt compelled to duck before it, but the golf course fence presents only a modest hurdle. In spring, Yellow Warblers delight in this place of extreme transition and pass readily over the obstacle. I thought of the dead goose as I looked at the golf course's barrier. Geese are not welcome on golf courses; they are chased from them. Could the goose's murderer have come from that side of the fence? Unlike the geese and the warblers, I have never felt an impulse to cross. However, the warning signs posted along the forest side of the barrier are not the deterrent to me. They read:

"No trespassing. $250 fine and/or imprisonment." Does not one incur both consequences if one enters the golf course from its main gate?

B-flat runs parallel to these signs along the fence for a time. But, again, I do not set foot on the golf course, for though in going from piano to Makamah I have traded one kind of circuit for another, the golf course is the most rigid and undesirable analog of the piano practice room—for the golf game has as its goal, too, that one take the fewest strokes to place small spheres in the right places.

One finds many golf balls in that area of Makamah's white-blazed circuit adjacent to the fence, especially after heavy rains. The golf balls are as the only arrowheads I have yet to find in this forest. I am told that I could find rare golf balls of an earlier design. These would be Archaic. I have only found modern golf balls, of my Woodland period. On the other side of the fence—as if with large hammers gripped by fingers—golfers seem to drive round fragments of white keys across a perfectly groomed, a perfectly tuned, field. No signs on the course side of the fence warn one away from the forest, and thus golfers send countless invasive white balls into the woods—as if trying to send pure seeds of C-major to where they are not welcome in B-flat. The white balls are as C-major melted into spheres from the plastic keys of cheap organs. The golf balls with stripes, of course, hint at inflections upon C-major, or perhaps they are fired in poor imitation of the warblers' freedom. Golf balls are a poor find for the woodland runner compared to an arrowhead. Golf balls have no sharp point, and they are also round and pale and dusty, like many who fire them. Their usually white color blends with almost nothing in the forest, except for snow, and when there is snow I presume not many golf-balls are newly lost. Yet finding one at any time is rarely an ancient discovery.

As Makamah's Circle of Fifths circuit moves slowly away from its brief parallel with the golf course fence, as I move away from B-flat and the hollow of the slain goose, I consider how two environments—one completely groomed, one completely unkempt—are pressed together for comparison. At first I consider the entire scene as one place as seen during two different times. It has been suggested to me that Makamah was once part of the golf course. I remain uncertain of that idea.

Yet I am certain that the golf course was at one time part of the woods.

But the sudden transition between the two in the present—no, the utter lack of transition; the lack of any sense of ecotone between course and forest—suggests something more: the image of the goddess-beast straddling a boundary; as the image of one piano, the dividing line running through its center, its keyboard split into two distinct registers by a landscape's border. The contrast is as of an out-of-tune register placed right next to a register that is subjected to constant service. The golf course is kept rigidly in tune by man, but directly adjacent to the course the forest's circle loses its connection to modern tuning by the season and with each succeeding year. On one side, the goddess-beast would endure an even burn; on the other, take an evolving tan.

F-Major (11 o'clock): The Ruin

By the time I make my arrival at F-major I see nothing without seeing it figuratively. For with F-major the thumb is engaged as of the first degree of the scale. The thumb—the head of the Runner as Giant Piano Hand—is first finger in an ascending scale at last. In F-major only one black key remains, and that seems embodied by the last superficial climb before the completion of the trail's net descent. This brief climb takes one to Makamah's only significant ruin—a foundation of considerable size and age, its stones showing no signs of having been mortared. Otherwise, the ruin consists only of a few slabs of concrete, posed at angles of dereliction, the concrete added perhaps at a later day, near what appears to have been the entrance to the vanished structure. Not a sign of its frame remains. The slabs lie in a jagged jumble, as if in complement to the two principal erratic boulders along the trail.

Each person to whom I have shown this ruin fails to match the speculation of any other when I ask a guest to imagine what once stood over this foundation. The ruin becomes as a triangular rock found by a desperate and inexperienced arrowhead hunter; so much false imagination is spent upon it. Somewhere in an archive, perhaps, a definitive answer can be found as to the form of the structure that once stood here. I hesitate to go looking in the files of the historical society.

When I pass this ruin I often recall recent visits to the playgrounds of my childhood. How fascinating are the indentations in the soil that commemorate the circles that enwrapped dismantled merry-go-rounds, the complementary landing points of vanished seesaws, and the touchdown points of dismissed slides. Grass returns to the places that had been under the shadow of the now-retired equipment, and new installations sometimes straddle the locations of the old, but these indentations remain. These indentations—these orbital trails engraved by the pointillism of tiny, vanished feet—remain after the key of gravity is removed; one carbon dates the great seesaw pits by the depth and recalcitrance of such holes; one imagines the cries from the children who formed these lasting landings, just as one listens for the imagined parakeet echoes from the Christmas tree of D-flat.

But are the past sounds that once emerged from such depressions lost forever? I suspect that they are not. Not too far from Makamah, in the forest surrounding the ruin of the great outdoor amphitheater on the old Rosemary Farm Estate in Huntington, I suspect there is preservation of even fleeting utterance. On the stage of that amphitheater John Philip Sousa's band is said to have performed, and Broadway names of that same time. Thus the carbonized breezes, the breaths of brass and woodwind players from more than a century ago, must surely be enshrined in the rings of now mature oaks, those rings like the grooves in a wooden 78. Thus the grazing bucks who feed on the acorns that litter the present backstage of that amphitheater: when they shed their antlers, is it as if they drop Edison cylinders? When I pick up a dropped rack, what march is recorded forever in its grain, or what verse of a flapper's ballade encased in its points? Far more is insinuated in an acorn than in the golf balls planted hopelessly in B-flat.

If a forest fire raged through the trees behind Rosemary Farm's amphitheater, would the blaze scrape away the matrix from the carbon fossils of the oaks, and would the crackle of the flames match the roll-offs of concerted snares, the charred trunks then revealing themselves for frozen stands of Washington Posts?

I suspect I have seen instances when trees have swallowed moments from my own present. Once, on a July thirtieth evening, by a rare and singular intensity of acoustic shadow, the sound of the concert band in Northport Village carried up into the wooded hills well above the park, but left a profound buffer of silence between its source and its reappearance amidst the trees where I stood. For a moment, from the darkening needles of evergreens came a magic ventriloquism, the orchestration interpolating an owl who was present in those trees. Did the acoustic shadow work both ways? Did the conductor on the bandstand in the village wonder who was hooting in the band? At that same moment the season of fireflies was at its peak, and their intermittent flashes seemed draped like stars on the branch stripes of the evergreens. Thus for a moment I saw a civil-religious Christmas in July, for I stood in a grove of Sousa Trees. I needed no parakeets, for the owl and the band had arrived. In winter I stand in the midst of these trees like the disaffected pianist as candle, hoping to hear and light this Sous-a-lantern again. I stand in the midst of these trees in winter like summer fireflies, as the eyes of jack-o-lanterns that have yet to find their skulls.

I have imagined already a piano straddling the border between the golf course and forest. An actual piano occupying such a position would rapidly go to ruin and disintegrate, leaving, at last, only an impression in the ground like the one that remains at F-major. I imagine at times that it was a vanished and vast grand piano that stood above that cellar hole. A grand piano with its lid removed—when looked at from directly above—can suggest the outline of a bordered garden, an empty swimming pool, or a landscaper's pond. But if that imagined structure above the cellar hole of F-major is as a piano with its lid still attached, then it hints at the appearance of an inverted box trap: the lid serving as the flat ground, the open piano as the box, and the stick as the stick. But what is the string of the box trap in that analogy and who held it and for what purpose? The purpose of the trap would be to catch the singing voices that emanated adjacent to it—voices of carbon-laden sighs that would be lost forever but for some containment. The figurative string of the trap was held by the memorializing trees that hunted on the edge of that imagined vanished structure, as did the trees on the edge of Rosemary Farm's amphitheater.

An actual piano in ruin, deep in the woods, I have not yet found. To find one would cause a profound reaction of wonder, for I always experience a subtle jolt, a sliver of unease when I have had the rare occasion to see any piano outdoors. Perhaps, as a pianist, I took up running—and then, further, running on trails—because one rarely or never expects to find outside that usually sheltered thing from which one wishes to escape. The climate-control devices applied by technicians seem to suggest that little of the flux of the outdoors should ever be around a piano. I have always noted the intimidation that comes from hearing one's own piano playing in the extreme reverberation of a large hall, after moving there from a dry space, like a small room or practice room. But the effect of playing upon a piano outdoors has a more unsettling effect. The concert hall's reverberation can cause a disturbance to the pianist's nerves and ego; but the sound of a piano outdoors is a disturbance as that of encountering something dead or even unnatural in the outer world. The piano is an instrument always presumed to be heard in a contained but resonant space.

The moving of a piano constitutes an event. Only rarely should it, or does it, come to us. One who would move a piano frequently is a sort of special fool. (When a piano meets with stairs it is balked, and with grand underlying reasons.) But one who does not carry a piano in suggestive recollection while standing up, walking, running—while free of it—is a fool of a worse kind.

Because a piano cannot be carried, its metaphorical influence as a recalled object—its weight alchemized into ether—is fostered. One cannot be a strolling pianist as one can be a strolling violinist. I can carry a violin into the woods, and I have— as I used to do as a child for the sake of pranks, to alarm neighbors on secluded private driveways. I could then make the violin sound a devil's fable in another's mind, but not so much in mine, for it was still a weight in my hands, an object that could not be interpreted because of such accessibility. A violinist walks out on the stage with his instrument; the pianist walks to or away from his instrument. One cannot recognize a pianist from what he carries. It leaves no discernable mark upon him. A piano, for instance, does not leave a bruise under the chin as does often a violin upon the neck of its player. A view of a pianist—and his view of himself—always compels one to recall a place to which he is not attached when he is walking. The piano is so stolid that a pianist must return to a place to return to it, and a piano is also almost always a place within a further place.

Some first implications from the piano's immovability came to me in a third grade music class. The teacher, Mr. Hedberg, had been introducing the grand staff on the blackboard. He asked how it was that I knew the notes so well. "Do you play an instrument?" he asked. "No," I replied sincerely. "Just the piano," I added. "Well, that's an instrument," said Mr. Hedberg. My impression had been that an instrument by definition could not be bigger than its player, that it had to be held, that it could be carried.

Yet that was a flawed conviction to hold before Mr. Hedberg, for he rolled a piano into the classrooms of the early grades. I remember the cheers upon his approach, as if a train were coming—not cheers for music class so much as for the sound of the piano's arrival: not its strings, not its music, but its rumble as an object—that piano not on casters but on the sturdy and framed institutional dolly trucks common to uprights in elementary schools. Were we thought too young to walk to his classroom? Or were we given the hint that some pianos might be wild and could move to us?

Perhaps the delivery of the first piano to my family's house had reinforced that hint. It was a large, Francis Bacon player piano, and it could not be made to pass through our front threshold. The railing of an inner stairway provided a formidable barrier. The memory of the delivery of that piano is of a day-and-night-long struggle, and the story perhaps suggested to me that something wild lived and remained even in such a complex machine— that the piano had had to be captured, corralled, and forced into captivity. I used that old piano into my teens, until there was almost nothing left of its action. That piano is gone now, and all that remains to me of it are a few yellowed shards of its genuine ivory—those shards on my desk, sharing a place with a treasured arrowhead and fossilized shark teeth.

It was during my later elementary school years that I had my last glimpse of a possibly wild piano in actuality. At Christmastime, on the edge of the harbor in my home village of Northport, I saw an upright on the back of an open bed truck on a weekday night. Mrs. Baldwin of the schools played it, and Mr. Krueger of the schools and community band was there, as well. They were both on the truck's bed, leading a crowd in Christmas songs for the lighting of the enormous cut tree just installed at the base of Main Street. The memory is a grand flash in my mind. The piano on that truck did not seem so unnatural as other outdoor pianos I have glimpsed in my life. Perhaps it was the cold night air that aided in this impression— as if there were little chance of mold to set in from a humid day, or sun to dry and warp the wood. The piano seemed native to the scene. It seemed a piano that must have been rereleased to a forest after the event. As some Christmas trees remain in-ground and are later brought back to the woods, then some caroling pianos may be returned to the forest to den near the vanished skirts of such evergreens.

When I think of the box trap imagery that

occurs to me when I am adjacent to the cellar ruin of F-major, and then ponder the imagined piano that might straddle the boundary between the forest of B-flat and the golf course, I wonder if the former is not trying to trap the latter—if one enfabled piano of the forest is not trying to catch another, and then at last itself or its own kind? My hopes suggest that there is yet a cryptozoological goddess-beast, a Klavier-Sasquatch roaming Maka-mah's woods. Sometimes I stand still and listen for it, but it is silent, not so as to hide from me, but perhaps so as to escape from its own sound. Yet still I pause and listen and often mistake for a moment the chance snap of the forest for the movement of the Klavier-Sasquatch. These are very subtle moments of aural confusion, like the fleeting instants while tuning into the radio wherein I mis-take the sound of a single guitar note or harp note for a piano's—the aural confusion in the woods always allowing one to keep some faith, prevent-ing one from ever concluding definitively that the woods are free of wild pianos. Sometimes when I pause on a warm day and listen to a distant roll of thunder, I wonder if an aged Mr. Hedberg leads a tethered Klavier-Sasquatch along the opposite side of the circuit—and if the sounds of the spring peepers are as third grade squeals at its approach.

I approach the woods each day with a hope (not with a vandal's hope but with a strange wonder) that I will find a derelict piano there, entrapped by the growth of trees, like the abandoned cars and couches I have found in Long Island's forests. Once, of a March seventh, in the pine barrens of Eastern Long Island, in the company of Mr. Klann, we crossed a woods road that had an abandoned couch on the side of the path. My trusted running friend wondered aloud how such a thing got there. "The wagon of an ATV?" I suggested—that ATV driven as if by Mr. Hedberg's warden counterpart in the eastern pine barrens.

But perhaps the car ruins that one finds from time to time in the woods are closer to what one hopes to find in a Klavier-Sasquatch. Of a February twenty-eighth, in woods much closer to Makamah than the pine barrens, Mr. Klann and I spent some time studying a common woodland car ruin—where the woods have grown up around the abandoned car, so that the derelict could not be wheeled out as it had been driven or pushed in long ago. This car ruin and the one not far outside the window to the left of the desk from which I now write (the latter in the woods above my native home, which I have seen and latently meditated all of my life) suggest something artificial that has been recaptured by the natural, made prisoner in a feral state of freedom. Before such cars were wrecks, they offered views of a speedily passing world; now, as ruins, these cars move only downward in particles at the speed of flaking rust. These cars no longer pass the landscape with speed; the landscape's trees now pass slowly upwards as they grow around the wrecks.

When I have come upon such ruins in the most advanced state of disintegration, when nearly all of the car has been mineralized, I have remarked that only a single tire is sometimes left in the end—evidence of that which had been in contact with the road.

Still I have not found direct signs of a Klavier-Sasquatch or of the goddess-beast. Yet what sustains my unshakeable faith? When I come across the smallest kind of impression left from ruins, when I double-back over my own course and see my own prints, I have unimpeachable proof, yet I can never study the prints and the maker at the same time.

In many forests, the sign of a former dwelling is often only a chimney. When I watched Mr. Hedberg lead us in song from behind his upright—or even when I have watched the silhouette of a concert pianist before his instrument in recital—does not the player suggest a vertical chimney set flush against the structure of the piano? Perhaps I am that chimney. Perhaps I am the moving chimney, last remnant of the most elusive ruin in the forest that I cannot find. The living chimney remains and runs, but the complementary instrument, the adjacent house frame, even its dent in the ground is harder to find with each passing year. This Klavier-Sasquatch is as certain and as common as the warbler in Makamah, yet I cannot watch him.

Thus it is I who pauses and listens each time I come abreast of Makamah's ruinous foundation of F-major, I the Klavier-Sasquatch, I the fabled box-trap, itching to immortalize fleeting strains? What success have I had as a hunter? Not long ago, of a May third, I heard, even in the midst of Makamah though coming from far off on the roads, the cycling jingle of the season's first ice cream truck. The ice cream truck's proclamation of "Turkey in the Straw" made its way clearly past the oaks to my own trapping ears. The tune of "Turkey in the Straw" had a life as a song in nineteenth-century minstrelsy, as "Old Zip Coon," yet after having its day on the stage and married to its lyrics, it wandered the backcountry with a case of amnesia. There it was sheltered by fiddle players and singers who nursed it back to life. The tune soon forgot, as well, its later marriages to newer lyrics, and today surfaces only as a tune. I have heard it whisper in obligato in the Finale of Charles Ives's Second Symphony. It wanders today like a sleep walker through the air. It came to me as lost as it did in the days at the end of its Minstrelsy. Or does the tune try to recreate its escape from commercial platform to the embrace of barn dance yet again, but now from ice cream truck to trails? Do I swallow the ice cream truck tune like the remote mountain fiddler, and thus leave the woods each day as a wordless man? If the tune reenters the forest via the chimes of the ice cream truck, as if to seek shelter yet again in a folk ear in a forest, then *I* am its box trap. I am as the memorializing oak and the chimney ruin. The fire of my own hearth would emit the song anew with the cremation-crackle of my bones.

And if, at last, these fires consume all but the last traces of my own ruins, perhaps all that will remain of me—rather as for the forest wrecks of cars—will be the like of a tire: the runner's forlorn shoe, his remaining rubber sole, the last ruin of him. The goddess-beast must succeed me.

C-major (12 o'clock): Wetlands Overlook

There is a considerable downhill from F-major to C-major. After a long stretch one moves past a small glacial erratic with almost geometric cuts on its top (perhaps a complementary and interlocking piece to a larger boulder that waits at the finale's hill at G-flat). But this smaller stone sits along a superficial uphill preceding the final descent, to where all is, at last, comprehensively level. Yet even on the edge of C-major—where all the black keys are gone—storms sometimes transpose that section with fallen branches, and one is compelled to make small leaps or climbs before reaching the lowest point of the circuit. Even when standing at the forest's edge abreast the shore of the Wetland Preserve, I have still turned my ankle from time to time, as when one catches the thumb nail in very rare instances in the cracks between white keys.

Only the water of the wetland beyond, reaching north and to the Sound, is truly level. When I have seen that water at its highest—of an April seventeenth—it covered the top of every reed and every strand of marsh grass. Yet almost always the marsh grass and reeds are visible. As that view of C-major comes into view for me, the wetland looks like a beard that can never gain but a consistently limited and whiskery growth. The shaving high tide never gives it a chance to grow to a forest's height, and the low tide marsh grass suggests a perpetual 5 o'clock shadow.

Sometimes a great tree at the edge of the marsh will fall and form a bridge to nowhere over the wetland. Recently I passed a young girl and a very young boy who had just climbed back from such a tree. As I ran by, I asked the girl, "How is the view?" "Beautiful," she replied. She had just been able to hover over the great level area of grass and water without stepping into it—this like having one's wrists and fingers resting over C-major without depressing the keys. To step directly into the marsh, however, is like depressing all the keys of C-major at once with one's forearm on a humid day. On an April day in 2013 in the company of Mr. Klann, I tried such an adventure and crossed the length of the marsh at low tide, only to learn that even the last evidence of my ruins were vulnerable to the suction of the mud, for I repeatedly had to kneel—level with the surface of where high tide would climb—to retrieve my lost running shoes. But perhaps they would be found at last, for years later I wrote a letter to the wife of a late high school music teacher of mine, a letter about arrowhead hunting. She replied, "Two of my brothers recall having arrowheads that a patient of my father's had found in the swampy area just before Crab Meadow Beach." That "swampy area" is the wetland of Makamah's C-major. But she concluded, "The arrowheads, themselves, have gone the way of all the other childhood things unfortunately." Yet it seems to me that "the way of all other childhood things" cannot provide greater concealment than a vast wetland—and even that wetland frees its prisoners, at last.

Still, the marsh water, the great level of C-major, acts as a deterrent to escaping the circuit at its lowest point. And when the tide recedes, when that plain seems to fall below the level of C-major, it is as if a key, a level, below the lowest is exposed but kept inaccessible. The marsh is like a moat to this end of the Circle but also a moat to itself. And beyond the marsh one is given a view of further barrier concentricities. Just to the right of the Crab Meadow Beach to which my teacher's wife referred, is a distant row of houses along the continuing shoreline with the Sound. From the sea wall of one of these houses, as he speculated a purchase, another running friend of mine, a builder, fell down to the hard rocks below and broke his pelvis in late November 2006, fell from that crumbling wall like a superstitious sea voyager might fear tumbling off the edge of a flat earth. Not until January sixth—while using a walker to complete one lap of a track—was my friend able to round a circuit again. I walked that first lap of his recovery with him and noted that by humiliations we must return to tight, tame, and level circles. From Makamah's marsh of C-Major, one can glimpse the latent encircling curves of the Sound, a view of a still further concentricity beyond the edge over which my friend had fallen—suggesting that in Makamah I am running a Circle of relative and inward minors in respect to these glimpses of greater outer belts.

It is at this point in the trail that one senses the inescapable turnaround of a circuit's trap. It is when I approach and pass through Makamah's C-major section that I feel the constancy of the Circle accumulating in a returning curve to the point of origin. The curve is as irresistible as the marsh boundary. This run and this essay are, at last, but efforts to escape and straighten this single, unceasing, curve. What remains in the Circle from hereon are scales that all begin with the thumb; the thumb (again, the head of the Runner as Giant Piano Hand) is now engaged first, before all the other figurative fingers. To become *all thumbs* is, at last, no diatribe.

G-major (1 o'clock): The Dead Raccoon

The wetlands still appear on one's left and command the eye, but soon it is apparent that the marsh will narrow into a creek as one slowly ascends in G-major. In early November, just after a rain, during night runs I have noticed that a certain kind of falling leaf leaves the newest layer on the forest floor. When the undersides of these leaves are exposed and dewed with rain, they give the appearance of tinfoil in the bright light of one's headlamp. These leaves then look like the wrappings that raccoons have thrown aside from their lunches.

At the same time of year and in the daylight I came across the carcass of a raccoon, in the center of the trail. Its tail suggested a chain of black and white keys encircling an axis, as if in oblique remark on the return of one black key in the scale with one's arrival at G-major. The body lay with its stomach down, limbs splayed out. It faced the same direction in which I had been running. I was hesitant, at first, to go so near as to pass the body, for it lay in such a lifelike pose I thought it might be playing dead. I had never seen a raccoon dead in the forest, not one in such perfect condition. I had seen many on the road, the victims of car accidents. When I meditate mortality and doubt the personal immortality of the soul, I often recall the sight of decaying animals in the woods. When I see the indifferent exposure of jaws and bones and inner parts that I know I have, as well, I often recall later that it was a dead raccoon over which I had lingered. Did this raccoon fall to its death? Such a fate seems unlikely: their climbing skills seem so great. But to lie right in the middle of the trail with no effort of concealment, and so lifelike in death! Perhaps an impact with a mountain bike at night? The sight put me in mind of Alexander Gardner's Antietam photograph: *Dead horse of a Confederate colonel, near the East Woods, on or about September 20, 1862*. Writes William A. Frassanito: "Its serene, lifelike pose startled many who, until close inspection, could not believe that the horse was actually dead."

Near the outbound end of another trail in eastern Long Island during the following late February, Mr. Klann and I noted a lovely young woman on an adjacent path, she wearing brightly colored running tights (almost of a brilliant, tie-dye pattern), and she was bending over the ground. She was midway between the trail we followed and the end of a dead end street. She could not have been more than twenty yards away, and I called out to her. She did not answer. "She didn't hear me?" I asked aloud. "I guess she's wearing headphones."

Mr. Klann replied, "She is burying a raccoon." He then speculated: Had she just found its body and thought it worthy of a decent interment? Or was she the murderer of a pest and hiding her crime? I wonder: Was she more discreet, if then burying a victim, than the possible murderers or murderesses of Makamah's goose and raccoon? How many recent or ancient murder sites have I passed unwittingly in the woods? Have I ever been a suspect myself and not known it? When Mr. Klann and I returned by the same path, the woman in the colored tights was gone.

During my lifetime I have observed as companies have added with increasing frequency their labels to the outside right of their pianos in addition to the traditional location of the lettering on the fallboard—especially on concert grand pianos: on the short, flat, area facing the audience, just before the start of the instrument's great and fertile curve. This new placement of the brand makes me suspect that this area is a piano's hip. From that lead I have been surprised that women's yoga and running pants have not yet taken to printing seductive text on the hip as well as the rear. Has any man failed to notice when a young woman in such pants drapes her hand at her cocked upper thigh, and her lithe forefinger extends down beyond the curve of her grip and suggests the slender stick that holds open the lid above a piano's now labeled hip? A piano's lid held at half-stick is as the goddess-beast bearing her midriff. The calculated rips in some women's jeans—sometimes at the knee or thigh—suggest a related chimney, lest the workings of the inner mechanics find no vent. To open a concert grand's lid is as to unlock a similar flue, and to see the stick's brass support cup is as to glimpse a pierced naval.

The woman who worked at burying a raccoon had worn running pants of a brilliant range of tie-dye colors (almost of a rainbow sherbet levity), thus making an affected play to an ungoverned nature developing within—as if laboring to suggest the reflection one can sometimes glimpse in the underside of an open grand piano's lid, of the raw inner workings of taut strings. But, at last, this woman seemed false prophecy of goddess-beast or Klavier-Sasquatch, for, in interring a raccoon, she appeared intent on hiding an emblem of nature's best effort to untune the trails.

In the very center of a trail somewhat west of Makamah, and in a still later month (in a June), I came across another dead raccoon for myself. But perhaps because of the time of the year, I had fore-warning, for quite some distance from the carcass on the rolling path, I remarked its carrion scent. The strong odor of such disintegration, emanating right from the path that marks a circuit, suggests the piano that is sliding out of tune. I often feel most comfortable practicing on an out-of-tune piano, or at least one that is slightly out-of-tune. I feel ill-at-ease in fact on a piano that has just been tuned, and I feel more relaxed after I detect the first com-promise to the supposed perfection. I think there is some connection in this to my relishing the earliest casualties of the year—healthy, green-leaf windfalls from the first strong winds of spring, this often in mid-May to early late-May in the woods.

But of dead raccoons, the one I discovered on the Makamah trail in November has left the strongest impression. Though I confirmed it for dead, I felt compelled to step around it and off of the trail, distorting—for the first time, to the slightest degree—the length of the circuit and the distance between points on Makamah's Circle of Fifths. The key points I describe on this white-blazed circuit do not appear at consistent intervals—they do not stand in strict analogy to perfect fifths apart—but their fixedness, their immovability as points, have rendered them in analogy to a tuned perfection over time. The decaying raccoon unsettled this. I relish how nature renders out-of-tune the well-tempered courses set and measured by Man. How else to explain the latent fascination one feels for the moss that appears on a neglected trail, or the weeds that appear in a neglected track, like the cinder fifth-of-a-mile track that idles behind my old Junior High School in Northport Village—those weeds to yield to saplings that can form trees if left alone, those trees to cause out-of-tune-ness to the perfect fifth-of-a-mile, causing a runner to dodge the trunks and add distance to the circle. And those trunks also push the surface up around them, causing grades, vertical additions to the formerly perfectly tuned loop. This last point suggests the fascination one can have for raised sidewalks that are allowed to grow banked and steep, permitted to enjoy grand and seemingly ancient upheaval adjacent to wide and rough-barked trees. I note how towns plant new trees with often inadequate margins of open earth around them in the midst of new sidewalks, and I am always disappointed when they remove such trees, often quickly, lest the trees raise the sidewalks or adjacent road. Such trees are removed to protect level surfaces. But perhaps the deeper prohibition against permitting trees to distort pavement is the avoidance of the cumulative distance created by chains of such vertical upheavals, of the signs of a natural tuning's imposition in a well-graded, well-mapped, well-tempered, world. In the forest, all the upheavals and unremoved obstacles are premonitions of natural overtones run regnant.

How to explain that a pianist would form this fascination for out-of-tune-ness? Nearly all other instrumentalists tune their own instruments; the pianist is almost never trained to do this. The piano has a cult of separate tuners. What does this do to the psychology of the player of an instrument which he himself cannot maintain? Does this create an ego problem in the pianist, as in a man who never makes his own bed? Or does it hint at the benign secret of a better role? Never teach a pianist to tune and one suggests to him he has a role in encouraging the return of wildness, of the seductively and suggestively ruinous. He becomes the out-of-tuner! He becomes as the forest ranger who monitors for excessive logging. And yet so many pianists grant constant rights to clear-cutters, to tuners. Other instrumentalists keep their instruments locked in a definite season and survey; the pianist alone learns to accept the alterations.

The history of keyboard instruments reflects an increasing stability of tuning. One moves from the fragile harpsichord to the iron piano and, at last, to electronic instruments that never go out of tune. But I find in the modern piano, in its sly admittance of disrepair and loosened intonation, the near-apotheosis of development. Thus, for me, the line of evolution: harpsichord to piano to Klavier-Sasquatch. I do not believe that pianos have been in our midst for so long that an independent population cannot be reintroduced into the wild.

The odor of that dead raccoon in November was subtle, and I only altered my course in the smallest way by stepping around it. But had I stepped over his carcass, I may have added a slight distance to the circuit, as well, a subtle new out-of-tune-ness to Makamah's Circle of Fifths.

Yet even when one steps over an obstacle in the trail, the human form seems by design at first to reinforce the status quo of tunings. I have noted while negotiating obstacles and making my way over roots, human legs suggest Salvador-Dali-esque distortions of bicycle wheels—that the function of our stride suggests liquid indentations within a wheel-shape that permits an obstacle, peg-and-hole fashion, to be bypassed with a level motion of exquisite smoothness. We run like spokes with no outer wheel. When the runner on the trail steps over objects without being raised by their height, when he can step over them in a fully adaptive stride, it is as if he has drawn the metaphor from the object. He is in tune with it. The runner's Dali-esque wheels have reacted yet have not been forced to alter altitude or direction from the obstacle. His legs react to its suggestion, but his full figure does not swerve or rise, this in parallel to a man's mind rendering an object into sympathetic metaphorical grist. He steps over it, frames and envelops the object without holding it or taking it in as material substance. For a moment he retains only its suggestion. The runner on natural ground with his Dali-esque wheels reads the uneven ground as if it were even. He stays level on unlevel ground. From obstacles that are too big to admit this effect, obstacles that compel a runner to jump or climb, comes the universal admiration for the equestrian, and for the deer that can move at a level gate through much of the forest. The teachers of many young pianists preach that one keep a level hand: the pianist's hand, then, as equestrian statue, as a rider on a doe negotiating roots in calm.

D-major (2 o'clock): Deer Curve

Despite the dead raccoon's hints of the circuit's unfixedness, I swayed little from the trail and moved onward to the altitude of two black keys. It is in Makamah's D-major that I have encountered an almost unavoidable obstacle to the circuit's fixedness. As I followed a hard right turn in the trail on one afternoon late in March of 2016—that bend just before the spot where some-one has restored a little in-ground Christmas tree to the right of the path—I faced a cancelling and equally hard left turn two to three yards ahead. In the center of that second turn stood a deer. The deer faced me and looked into my eyes. I am uncertain why he did not retreat before my arrival. Was I so quiet because alone? Did the noise of wind in the forest cover my approach? I wonder if he thought a true threat would only approach in a straight line? The right turn I had taken to face him is sudden. Had he seen me from afar—when I was on the straightaway where in 2017 I would find the dead raccoon—and thought that I was on a course to miss him? I have noted on very gnarled mountain bike trails that deer will often let one pass very closely in parallel motion when two parts of one curvy trail come into adjacency, but they will rarely let one approach them directly on a straightaway. Though deer seem to use trails—their scat gives the evidence of this to me—they seem never to use them as a means of flight from a person. And when I run on winding mountain bike trails, the bushwhacking deer will sometimes escape the trail and then stop at a point in flight that holds a narrower lead from me than when I had met them at the original point of threat. Do they feel satisfied then that one is not on a straight line of attack but following the trail? Are they capable of this kind of reasoning? What forest geometry do the deer practice?

When I see the deer of Makamah on my runs, I recollect my reading that contends that white tail deer evolution is shaped by their interconnectedness with wolves. Wolves have been gone from Long Island for centuries. I wonder what collective troubles the deer suffer without the presence of wolves. What of Man without his own respective wolves? And yet perhaps the wolves remain on the circle, after a fashion. For the deer flee at the sight of a seemingly pursuing man, and yet surely the deer are not conditioned to flee from a running man because they associate him with stationary bow hunters; today they must equate Long Island mankind principally with handouts. But the running man suggests something to them—reminds them of a threatening pressure even when that pressure is gone. Thus is not the idea of a Wolf Man an actuality at that moment? The tails of the deer go up in flight, aping the full moonlight necessary for my transformation. The Universal Studio monster is a universal monster at that moment.

But this deer of D-major! He made me stop. I say *he*, for though he had yet no antlers at that season of the year, he seemed bold and aggressive as a buck, hesitant to yield the trail's ground. He pointed the opposite direction from the dead raccoon that would come to characterize G-major for me. As I remained still, I meditated changing direction on the circuit, or of bushwhacking a wide bypass of his claim. I called out, "Hello!" He backed off of the trail at last and moved closer to another deer that stood just a few feet into the trees. After he stepped off, I passed, and both deer bolted into the inner forest of Makamah's circle.

Had he fled from me in autumn, I would have seen a trail system summarized in foreground, middleground, and background in close relief: the tail, when raised, suggesting a tree blaze on the trail in one's foreground; the spine representing the path itself in the middleground; the antlers suggesting the forest beyond in an inviting background. The buck carries a diorama of the forest circuit on his back, and to come upon a set of shed antlers is as to come upon the background of the forest close at hand, yet with the trick of scale exposed.

But my challenger had accomplished a great deal more in suggestion, even more than the dead raccoon—though, at last, he did not force me to go around him. There is much grist in the moment when one is compelled to yield the trail to another— to step aside and sense the circuit hanging over the precipice of out-of-tune-ness, to sense that the trail's distance is augmented when one defers to a fellow traveler. The runner who steps aside, say, even for a moment into the interior of the circuit, becomes as a relative minor. One also steps aside at times on a loop to those who suggest a stronger motion from the opposite direction—to those who suggest dominant motion to one's subdominant motion. Not long ago, late in November, on a trail near Makamah, I stepped aside for two groups—the second not far behind the first—of middle school cross-country boys. Toward the end of the second and smaller group's passing, I started to grow impatient with the consistent ingratitude of each boy. But just when I was ready to form an opinion of this team, one of the last fellows in the line thanked me for stepping aside. When I do not step aside in such instances, and both parties pass the other closely in opposite direction, I am reminded of tabletop pieces attributed to Mozart, works for two violins, written on a single piece of paper yet read from opposite sides of a flattened stand or table. Tabletop pieces suggest the ineradicably different look of a trail depending upon the direction of travel. To one looking both ways on a trail while stopped, one sees that the two directions, even on a circular path, are not commutative. Just as the interval of a fifth in music (say, C to G) transforms into a fourth when inverted (G to C), just as the clockwise Circle of Fifths becomes a Circle of Fourths when one reverses direction, a trail viewed in a new direction is an entirely different path. One cannot retrace one's steps.

Yet when I stand still and yield to opposing and faster traffic, the other parties do not realize how much I sacrifice. So much of what one sees on a run is not seen on a walk or from the most picturesque stationary point of vantage. For a run, however untimed, has a tempo and an implied fabric of continuity that seems to link ostensibly unrelated objects with greater frequency for me than all other forces that foster association. I have noted that a study of the forest often benefits as do some printed texts: from a faster rate of reading. Brisk tempo is often required to activate a chain of syntax and to comprehend some styles. One cannot jog a mile a day and after 26.2 days be credited for completion of a marathon. The thumb must pass quickly to solder a scale. The brisk and unceasing legato of the Runner as Giant Piano Hand forms the impression of a snow angel. The deer and I are always running when we meet.

A-major (3 o'clock): Steve of Makamah

Even after hints from the dead raccoon and the deer, I stick to the course of the trail. I move to A-major and reach again a count of three black keys and more altitude. The circuit leads me to where the great marsh on the left narrows into a pond. It would be as thin as a creek here but for a dam. Two side trails intersect with the white-blazed trail at this point, including one from the interior of the forest and one that follows the spine of the dam. On two consecutive days (May sixth and seventh of 2019) in this intersection I encountered the same man at the same time of day, he moving in the same direction (counterclockwise) both times. The man seemed fixed to A-major, or was himself the defining feature of that part of the circuit.

One month later (on June sixth), I saw the same man in the same place again. As I started to ascend the rise just past the causeway that dams the creek, the man came into view again.

"We always intersect at the same place!" I exclaimed.

"I know," he replied, as I ran by.

"I'm Jack!" I called out, and I continued on.

"Steve!" he shouted, since we were parting back to back.

On June 19 I ran into the same man on a different part of the trail for the first time—in this instance at the base of a great hill, near the end of B-major and just before the ascent to G-flat.

"Steve!" I exclaimed, with a slight inflection to embrace the possibility that I could be wrong.

"What was your name again?" he replied as I passed.

"Jack!" I answered.

On December fourth, while passing through A-flat and the Valley of Oaks in the company of Mr. Klann, I spotted a figure in the distance, coming from the opposite direction, approaching us perpendicularly because of a bend in the same path. "Sasquatch!" I announced to Mr. Klann in hopeful jest. When the putative beast was close I recognized Steve yet again.

Once more I began with, "Steve!" He replied affirmatively but looked puzzled. I explained that he had seen me running earlier in the year and usually in the same spot or near it. I was more bundled up on this day and wore a winter hat. He recognized me at last, it seemed. He smiled and moved on.

On December fifteenth I saw Makamah Steve in yet two new places on the circuit on the same day. Two people must be repeating the same form in order to see one another more than once even in a small forest. As I descended from B-flat's parallel with the Golf Course, I found Steve off of the trail to my left, he making his way clockwise through the dead leaves. "I'm looking for my lost golf ball!" he joked after I hailed him by name again. He had become chatty and friendly, though he did not use my name nor ask to be reminded of it again. I saw him the second time that day, on my second loop, in the same place I had seen him on June nineteenth, just before the ascent to G-flat. He asked if I knew who had painted the new blazes of yellow arrows, this path sharing some parts of the white circuit but not all.

"Moutain bikers?" I speculated.

Seeing Makamah Steve in increasingly varied places—after first forming the impression that he seemed fixed to one location—made him seem as the first emblem of a shared template to all keys on this circuit. Or was he always in the same place, and does the Circle spin?

I saw him last on January sixth of 2020. I saw him three times that day. At our third meeting on that one run I exclaimed, "A first for us! A third overlap!" I do not think it suggested as much to Steve of Makamah as it suggested to me.

I note my compulsion to alter slightly the greetings of each encounter. I remember feeling embarrassed during recitals before audiences constituted principally of musical laymen, wherein large sections of a piece, as in a sonata-form, are repeated verbatim (*note*batim?), with the expectation that the performer must make some subtle effort by articulation to distinguish and justify the repetition for such an audience, as if to allay their likely boredom—while the professional listener is trained to accept that the repetition is an ostensibly high obligation of the form. But notwithstanding my knowledge of the latter, and my efforts to render the former, my embarrassment always left me with a latent urge, as if to say something to a lay audience as I do to people I pass more than once on a circuit of a trail. I never wished to say something foolish and wry like, "Here we go again!" But I have wished to cry out, "Hello again!" in cheerful earnest.

There is something profound to me in the "Hello again!" in the cyclic running context— and that it occurs usually at different places each time in the loop because both parties are moving. Indeed, both parties were moving in all the recollections I give above. There is a study in this: building an implied knowledge of another person or object without compromising that knowledge by entering the artificial territory of augmented contact time. In this light, the repeated exposition in a sonata-form movement starts to seem a sign of a composer's mistrust, and perhaps this applies to repeat signs of all kinds and to all unnecessary italicization in conversation, all our fears that our point has been missed. I seem to run by all my best alliances without a pause. Composers— and perhaps Music itself—seem to mistrust that we can catch salient details in single and speedy passes. I believe we catch things the first time and only pretend to forget the names of those we have passed on the trail.

I have seen Steve of Makamah in nearly all places on the white-blazed Circle of Fifths, just as I have noted that raccoons, deer, tree carvings, dead animals, moon shadows, appear on all places on the Circle. Nothing that seems indicative of one location does not at last seem to migrate in disguise along interior lines. When an impediment greater than a dead raccoon or a stubborn buck—something like a fallen tree trunk—puts the trail's course in disarray and pounds a hole into the ground from its fall, does it not seem that the very ruin of F-major appears to travel? A pianist starts to note that distant keys on the Circle of Fifths often share the same fingerings; pianists are even encouraged after a time to import fingerings between distant keys that do not share them. Physical modulations increase as the Circle's rigidity becomes uncertain. All scales, at last, can be started on a thumb.

I have not seen Steve of Makamah since January sixth of 2020. But I have almost encountered myself on repeated loops. On January eighteenth I went for a run in a new, light, afternoon snow. I saw no signs, save for animal signs, of prints in the snow as I began. When I reached the final crest of the yellow access trail—and could see across to the white-blazed circuit on the opposite, slightly lower, plateau—I noted that the snow had heavily outlined the distant trail in profound relief against the adjacent and ublazed parts of the forest, even though there was snow on the ground everywhere in the woods. The snow was evidence of God dusting for fingerings. For a blazed trail presumes a predecessor; it is as a score written by a blazer, a composer, of the way. The subsequent runner is merely as the pianist, the recreative performer, following the way—at best marking the snow with his footprints, with his newer figurative fingerings. The blazed trail under new snow is as a minimally edited edition, as an urtext under the runner's weight.

I ran two loops that day, but the snow fell enough that I did not encounter my own prints until I reached B-flat and the edge of the golf course a second time. My earliest prints had been erased. But if one runs two loops in a forest in snow, one cannot help but encounter some of one's own fingerings. On snowy days I sometimes catch myself stepping involuntarily as best I can into another's tracks, as if they possess authority, like editorial fingerings, as if Paderewski or Percy Grainger had run the trail before—as if a recreation of those steps with faith is as important as following the trail, the figurative score, itself. Yet, as on my second loop of that January eighteenth, I found it hard to land precisely even in my own tracks—suggesting what it feels like to practice scales repeatedly around the Circle of Fifths on a piano that is going rapidly out of tune.

But a heavy snow falling on one's repeated circuits of a trail allows the best realization of Debussy's injunction that we must look for our own fingerings, even against our recent own. Yet even on the days of the heaviest snow, I follow the trail. But the reader may bushwhack in this essay and enter at his choice anywhere in the circle's bend.

E-major (4 o'clock): Tree Carvings

I follow the painted blazes. During the longest days of the year, however, the brilliant and almost horizontal light of the long evenings sends temporal blazes by the hundreds into the darkening woods. These patches of white light are as timed blazes on the trees—blazes that seem to proclaim:

"Look here, where you have never looked before and may never look again!" These are blazes that exist for themselves and lead to themselves. Most of the time the timed blazes illuminate with great white light the barest square of bark, a space no bigger than a baseball base or a notebook's blank page. The evening light in earliest summer brings the blank but brilliant pinups and renders the forest into a locker room of blinding Miss Junes. No man would flip forward in this calendar, but this month lasts only minutes on the bark. As if trying to immortalize such pages, I have noted that vandals will sometimes draw little faces into the painted blazes on the circuit, but these cannot be lighted into jack-o-lanterns, for the trees cannot be illuminated from within. But hints of possibility thrive, as when on a night run one looks up with a headlamp and sees raccoon eyes looking back and moving—like Betty Grable eyes that will not stay put on the nose of a warplane.

By the comprehensive light of noon, however, one runs the woods as if witness to a theater production, for no matter the effort of that play's Director, one cannot be forced to look at the place on the stage the Director chooses. It is easy to redirect one's gaze, to let an object or person of one's choice draw focus. Thus the bright and equalizing light of noon is somewhat ungodly, for I am made director by the freedom of my eye. While I was seated at a rehearsal piano, I once heard an actor remark, "Nothing says revue like chaser lights." Nothing says bushwhack like noon sun.

But in the late-May to late-June light of evening in the woods, God commands the eye with a cinematic despotism and not with the limited grip of the playhouse. The timed blazes are as the pointed camera of God and not a mere follow-spot.

Yet still I follow the painted blazes of the circuit with devotion. Studying them has led me to note other markings of Man on the trees. On a day in April I passed a tree that has come to haunt the A-major section for me. Carved into its bark is the date *3/27/05* (some carved dates are more important than any carved initials). I passed the tree on subsequent runs having learned with disappointment that my own journal showed no entry for this date. I felt as if the carvers had a claim to that day on the calendar—that they had lived it, and I had lost it. To boot, they had spent it in my native place while I recalled that I had passed it in a brief period during which I had lived in another part of the state.

Each time I passed this carving soon after, I continued to amplify the imagined advantages the carvers enjoyed. Would not the carving continue to climb over the years, as if God put his toe at the bottom of the youngish tree (like one who put a foot at the tripod base of an adjustable music stand), and pulled the stand up to his level of sight? Is the carving as writing that may rise into the infinity of the forest canopy, like the text in the opening crawl of *Star Wars* or of a Flash Gordon serial, though much more slowly? As the tree grows, does it change the placement of the carving's line as if to a higher place on a score—as if it places the carving in another instrument's voice, as if it changes the orchestration? Does the tree place slowly the aspirations of the carving lovers out of reach, as if the tree or God thinks the carving dangerous for them and others and puts the carving on a higher shelf? Do such trees serve like headstones turned into stalagmites?

But one learns that this cannot be so. Trees do not grow in such a way as to support this fancy. The collected tree carvings of a forest suggest a gallery wherein the only surviving bits of art are the vain signatures in low corners of the canvases, from painters who left no paintings, who dared to claim God's work of the tree for their own. One notes some rare carvings that are much above those that cluster at a man's height, but because the carvings are of recent date, it is evident that a ladder had been used, or some other means for climbing. Carvings climb high not by a tree's growth but when carvers run out of blank bark. Other ostensible carvings above the height of human reach turn out to be anomalous natural scars; the passing misconception bred from seeing these natural engravings is like the brief and excited confusion of the novice arrowhead hunter upon finding triangularly shaped or broken stones.

On night runs, only the moon rises up as if attached to the microphone stands of the trees. The moon is like a microphone head pulled up by taller and taller singers. The moon may start low and learn and light the music score of the bark carvings. But as the revue ghosts of the forest grow taller, the score is left low, and the microphone is pulled up high by those who sing only by memory.

But the bark of the trees can alter the carvings in a suggestive way. Not many yards before *3/27/05* and its tree is a tree with the carving *FRANK + HELEN*. Frank and Helen left no date—for perhaps they were confident in the eternal values of honesty and classicism—and their carving remains very much at the height it occupied when it was created. But the growth of the tree's width with age fosters the slight expansion of the letters and the distance between them—like newsprint distorted on stretched Silly-Putty. Perhaps those augmentations are evidence that the Klavier-Sasquatch has left its mark while sharpening its claws on the bark—leaving a mark of territorial out-of-tuneness on the illusion of a rigid circuit.

Again, I left no journal entry myself for March twenty-seventh of 2005; I blinked. But I think it is a safe guess that I went running that day.

B-Major (5 o'clock):
Arrowhead Creek

When one reaches B-major, all five black keys are again in play, but one still starts this scale with the thumb. The combination of elevation and mind are near their zenith.

The great marsh of C-major is constricted into a narrow creek not far off the left side of the trail by the time one reaches B-major. And B-major's end swerves away from the creek to begin the steepest climb of the entire circuit. As I have passed that creek before the great climb, I have often thought of the times that I have hunted it for arrowheads. Any worthwhile academic study will compel one to fold one's body. Save for the blessed time that I have been able to stand, walk, and run, I have had to fold my body upon the piano benches of the world. For some time now I have had joy in taking respite from practicing the piano, from keeping my foot and leg chained to the damper pedal, the latter obligation causing the same ache that a long-distance drive brings to the right leg of a motorist. But engage in the study of one's predecessors in any way (in this case the search for arrowheads, objects that encouraged their makers, at last, to stand upright and straight) and one seems folded upon a piano bench again.

Like the creators of the arrowheads, we start with our own figurative chipping and carving, and our best works are rarely discovered at the place of their submission or composition. One can never fix the spot of the best time capsule or shrine. And in the firing of our figurative arrowheads—our self-promotions and publications—we rarely accomplish much. But in the actual and the figurative arrowhead's case it is often the missed shot, the ostensibly lost and forsaken firing, that is most free to have the time and freedom to drift, to find the most sympathetic hand and eye at last. The arrowhead is valued most then if intact, for those who make the future discoveries have the least desire to pare down and editorialize.

The life of an arrowhead suggests that one may blink slowly at times yet miss nothing. An arrowhead is as the opposite of a vain tree carving. An arrowhead is an unsigned masterwork that has drifted downstream from a lost gallery. An arrowhead is such a spare artifact—no shaft, no feathers, no binding remain—that one only discovers a stone that praises our impulses in the present. It brings no reinforcement from the past but a sign that its maker cannot act in the present, cannot leave a mark to contradict the present belief that the revealing creek is more stones, water, fish, and reflected sunlight than importuning monument. Finding an arrowhead hardly assures the finder that one even had a predecessor; perhaps that is the confounding joy in finding one. An arrowhead has all the suggestiveness of a ruin yet proves no real antecedents. I am often indifferent when I find no arrowhead, for in looking for them one is leaving one's own. An arrowhead is an historical district that does not tell me how to build my new house. It is as an artifact that resembles what is already there in the creek: fallen leaves and triangular stones. Always run as an original settler.

Leaves in the stream often fool me into thinking I have found an arrowhead. I am drawn into the creek to look more closely, but I am still a prisoner of the circuit and subject to B-major when I do so. Ice flowing down such a creek resembles a traditional treadmill. Gravity is the motor of the band. But the summer creek is as a magic treadmill, where the band is not met by one's soles but by one's ankles, even by the thighs and waist where and when the band is thick. The creek is as a treadmill through which one can reach through its rolling deck. It is cold to the first touch but at last undetectable as to temperature. It is reflective and invisible in succession. One cannot control its incline or speed. This band is longer than any that fits in a gym. Fish live and move in this band. They often run its length themselves and remain stationary as the band rolls on. One's sweat does not dot this band; it joins it. Under the hot sun my brow adds mass to this treadmill. Deer and other animals drink from the band and thus ingest a pace or tempo, even drink a course itself. If one suddenly stops moving on such a treadmill, one does not necessarily fly off the back of the band. If one goes up a dry tributary, it is as running on a treadmill that has been unplugged, or on one from which the band has been removed. The intersection of two running creeks, however! That point is as marvelous as if two adjacent treadmills could blend their bands at oblique angles and at different speeds! On rainy days such treadmills appear in the streets, and their bands disappear into storm drains. During a great rain in 2004, such a watery band washed away the finish line mat of Northport's 10-K race. The implication then was that the course had been reversed and its distance made infinite?

Should one find an arrowhead in any creek, I advise, in honor of the vigil and the drift the object has performed, that one blink slowly upon first sighting it, and blink slowly upon picking it up. Yet somehow my runs remain uninterrupted, and the circuit holds one to its course and the inevitable last climb.

G-flat: Tattoo Girl and the Erratic

The return to G-flat and to the highest point on the circuit demands the steepest ascent of the run. As I climb this great hill, Makamah's Circle of Fifths, like a cooper's hoop, still strains to keep the white-blazed trail tight and in tune. I have heard it said that the Cosmos is expanding. Does God inflate that balloon? I know that I am most out of breath as I ascend this final hill at a run. Does Makamah's balloon get bigger, the most out of tune, at last, from all of my puffs? If I walked the hill I would be little threat.

On a recent May ninth as I reached the base of this steep hill the tender spring leaves impressed me with the intensity of their greenness, but I was pleased to know that they were not yet at their peak. For though the peak may be more intense in color, it is, at last, the peak: the point of apotheosis. But to be overwhelmed at the base of this hill by the greenness of the leaves while still in their immaturity, was as to pause for an instant in an illusion of perpetual ascent, to fancy that there is no apotheosis, that there is always more intense green yet to come. For a brief instant it is as to have no certainty of even the year's circuit.

Yet one must at last reach the top of the hill and the close of the Circle. Again, with B-major the maximum count of five black keys was reached again, and on reaching G-flat a second time, one cannot find a sixth black key. The Runner as Giant Piano Hand cannot be raised further.

At the top of this hill, not far from the intersection where one began the circuit, is Makamah's largest erratic boulder. That rock was dropped by the vanished glacier slope, as if there the ice gave up on the dream of perpetual inclines above the crust; gave up forever, and now the glacier's mighty continuance of incline pools down only as a ghost, as that humble creek one can search at B-major.

But I say: Stand on that erratic and choose neither left nor right! Do not submit to the mere Circle again! Cry out a single tone in thy breathlessness! Think no more of scales and key signatures, nor of formal pitch collections that can be found on any keyboard. The Circle of Fifths is a straight line that has been forced back on itself. Stand atop that stone and reject left and right, and note the infinite tower instead that is said to accumulate by Nature over a single pitch: the Overtone Series—that series climbing ceaselessly upward with rungs that are uniquely spaced, a ladder that cannot bend into an arch but must move out straight, for from its infinite length it cannot bend! It is a ladder decreed by Nature with perpetual strength against curves, against the flaccid.

Only the perpetual ascent remains, as that of the eternally outbound rocket, as a comet with no orbit. Circles seem to require some external force to create them, and an external influence to maintain them in figurative tune. Such shapes must be cultivated, as the curves of grand pianos are achieved by strict braces, and as the bends are imposed on boundary trees in the forest. I still come across the latter in the forests of Long Island today. They suggest the right sides of grand pianos that grow from out of the soil. The Klavier-Sasquatch may grow from a seed than be born from a mammal's womb.

Though the crags of this great erratic boulder have at times appeared in interlocking complement to those of the smaller stone that one finds at C-major, this rock at G-flat seems as a period to the endlessly curved sentence of Makamah's white-blazed circuit. But it also seems a lonely and hinting semi-colon to the clause of ascending ice that once sloped above it—that vanished incline suggestive of perpetual ascent, of a Perpetual Preluding. That erratic boulder is as a massive glass Christmas ball planted by the trimming hand of God.

When I reach the level and then descending ground just past this boulder, I catch my breath and slow to a jog. In that stretch on a recent June eighth—a warm but dry day that was cool in the shade—the sun lay brightly dappled all over the forest floor. The forest canopy on such a day is as a sifter or screen one may use to hunt for arrowheads of shadowed light. It filters out the blinding sunlight as a screen in the creek removes the plain sand; it reveals glistening points on the forest floor—points that cannot be picked up; or patterns for points that are yet to be carved. Who might collect such patterns or points? I thought then of the running woman I had passed in this stretch on the preceding February eighth. She had a very slight stoutness that in an extremely fit woman is not unbecoming, and in addition to long and crow-black hair she had something about her Mediterranean skin, even in the paleness of winter, that made it clear she would easily and beautifully absorb a tan. I thought of her taking a tan from the dappled days of June sunlight in Makamah, and submitted to myself that her beauty and fitness and impressionable tenderness of skin might not just take a mortal tan, but a tan in high burlesque of those who burn in bathing suit patterns by poolsides. For her skin seemed that it would take both the dappling of the light's patterns, yet move, too, with the waving shadows of the leaves—her skin showing an olive pattern as of a tattoo that could realize a motion picture: her skin covered with moving tattoos. And then one imagined that they would fade away in winter, like neglected silent films that have escaped efforts of conservation. She is not as the desperate who commit to early drafts and live in resistance to revision (save from the slow redaction of wrinkling). Common tattoos are stationary like carved initials in the bark of a tree.

I have not seen her again. She alone would seem the fit Klavier-Sasquatch to climb the overtone ladder atop the erratic boulder of G-flat. She would reach with ease above the ladders that mortals must use to carve signs of their false romances in the trees. This Tattoo Girl, this true goddess-beast of Makamah, need wear no fallboard logo on her tight clothes, for the pattern is on her skin. The sincerity of her tattoos mock our attempts to restore the fallen autumn leaves in winter, as when we hang colored glass spheres upon Christmas trees. I believe the ornaments that trim the trail trees are in offering to her.

Conclusion

As I descended and came close to the end of the yellow access trail in a recent early March—at the time of year when the woods are still silent—I suddenly heard a bright and solitary bird of spring, far behind me, back in the midst of the circuit. First it suggested to me the sound of the Juilliard of the avian dinosaurs in morning time. But then it came to me like a sound from practice rooms one has already passed and confirmed as empty in the early hours of a holiday at a University—a sound that suggests that someone is indeed there, yet has remained unseen and unheard from one's sole walk through the empty halls. Some unseen presence always remains behind in the circuit, the solitary bird acting as the hinge squeak of the goddess' practice room door.

Such a lone bird's sound is as finding a lighted candle still burning in the bottom of a November first jack-o-lantern. One finds small insects entrapped in the low rings of the spent wax. But then, again, I swallow bugs myself when I am running. On my own porch I have slipped on traces of this hardened wax even in spring, just as I have fallen on the trail from time to time—as if tripping over signs of the presence I have yet to see but am sure is there.

Further along the descent of the yellow access trail I have often muttered: "A second growth forest is a pasture in benign ruin, going out of tune. More than lamenting to the young, 'Here, when I was young, was a forest and now a field!' is to boast, 'Here now is a forest where once was a pasture in ruin.'"

On autumn nights I return to the parking lot at the end of the yellow trail. I look back to Pebble Hill and recall my child self of 1973, even then caught in the circuit of the Flushing courtyard's walkway and in the mootness of left or right, locked in practice cycles before I ever touched a piano.

I who have run twenty-mile workouts on tracks and circuits know well the dread of a single lap's close—that end followed only by another start, akin to facing the first minute of a new practice session after logging a full, productive, exhaustive practice day on the day preceding. But I have dreaded less the treadmill on successive days. For even in starting a new day in a chain of treadmill days—and setting its grade to 2.0 to account for the absent wind—it is always as if a new sum has been calculated to a perpetual ascent to a Perpetual Prelude. By coincidence, the father of my kindergarten friend Josh once approached me when I was on a gym treadmill during a twenty-mile training run in winter. "What do you think about during all that time?" he asked. I wear no headphones, and I have no book on the treadmill's stand. I replied that I think the same things I might think during the passing of any equal amount of time. But there! There I perpetually ascend. There I am forever outbound. That was my answer to him. And these written remarks are my report to my mother and father. For they cannot watch me in the woods as they did in the courtyard when I was small.

Backphrasing: Musical Theater and the Newtonian Clock

I prize the unbidden ideas that have grazed my consciousness obliquely during piano perfor- mance and practice, over any work of music lit- erature or music lore. One of the most arresting suggestions came to me as a result of the challenge of switching as an accompanist from classical play- ing (as for art songs) to working for musical the- ater singers in concert settings. The first not only has the pianist and voice often locked together in strict doubling in the same register for melody, but compelled to remain yoked together as to tempo. Any rubato initiated by the classical singer is to be shadowed perfectly by the classical pianist, such that singers value a pianist who also breathes in synchronization with them. But in musical theater, while the singer retains almost all rights to rubato, the accompanist is obligated to remain in nearly strict time. The musical theater singer is expected to backphrase: to have the liberty to land on notes well after the written complements to those notes have sounded in the accompaniment. Yet outside of cliché's—repeating to me the expectations of the style—I have never heard a Broadway-credited performer tell me why it is they backphrase.

Though I had heard backphrasing all of my life, it was not until I was in my late thirties, and taking piano work where I was finding it anew, that I had occasion to play for theater singers. My first experience came with significant stakes, for the concert was assembled in haste, with only the afternoon before the evening performance for rehearsal. The singer was not yet in her gown, but she carried the invisible deed that comes with performers who have originated roles in shows of fame.

She stood in the center of the stage, microphone in hand, and I sat at a small grand piano, placed parallel to the edge of the deck. The singer was an intimidating display of Darwinistic power to my heterosexual eye, and with the authority of having sung before audiences that neither the pole of Art music nor the pole of popular culture can win, but before the wide and uncertain equatorial latitude that can be found best in a musical theater audience—where brows are both high and low, such that one can never dictate their average features to a sketch artist. She had had to sing for audiences of unknown sympathies that had to be won in the moment, they grabbed by an isolated personality working in great part without collective assistance. She had had to entertain.

We were rehearsing the song "My Man"—and rendering it in an arrangement that suggested the one used in the film "Funny Girl." The start of a new phrase approached, yet I heard no telltale breath suggesting to me that the singer was going to land on the next appointed beat written in the music, so the veteran art song player in me hesitated, and I held back a downbeat and felt I displayed a subtlety of response indicative of great musical skill. And, foolishly, in that same instant, I felt I had broadened the fan of my figurative peacock feathers before a beautiful woman. In my consciousness—all this played out in a silent, featureless, moment that started to gain neverthe-less a texture as that of a forming topography—I felt like one of a party of two, both of whom do not wish to reach a door before the other, but for different reasons. Think, then, of the effect for the backphrasing singer, caused by an accompanist who tries to wait for her, though she wishes to remain behind: one might almost reach a negative tempo, more than a standstill, yet not coursing backward!

She stopped singing and looked across to me.

"You're waiting for me," she said, and her words sounded through the PA in the house, for she did not lower the microphone. She said this with what I took to be a polite contempt, an irritation over my misplaced courtesy, a courtesy that translated to a confession of inexperience.

I felt embarrassed yet indignant at the same time. I sat on the bench like a frozen, cleaned, turkey. But the indignant part of me thought: She does not realize why I fell into a classical snare during her backphrasing, a trap of trying to live in complementary motion to her rubato, rather than remaining in a steady and independent motion. In such moments, I feel like musical theater singers are like sharks that want pilot fish but take exception if the pilot fish swim in perfect complement to their host.

I understood what she had wanted and what I had failed to give. She wanted the right to fly like a bee around a steadily moving runner, or like a dog that knows how much slack it can take on a leash so as to linger behind on a steady walk before being pulled. She wanted the right of the uncommitted lover in a romance: the partner that only races back when the other, steady, party becomes intolerant of the ambiguity. But I wanted her to know and concede the wisdom of my action. I wanted her to confess a degree of her own embarrassment in light of the countless analogies that then sprang to my mind in the endless width of that narrow moment of consciousness.

I thought of Virgil Thomson's first remark when asked by David Dubal to describe the Paris of the 1920s and 1930s:

"To begin with, nobody had telephones. There were telephones in business houses and hotels. But almost nobody you knew, except a few rich people, had telephones, so that you had a little black book in your pocket, and every time you met your friends, or rather every time you said goodbye to them, you took out the little books and made a date and wrote it down to see them the next time, and you kept that date. Nobody changed his opinion. If you did, it was an emergency. You sent a little telegram, a little blue telegram, called a pneumatique."

But the backphrasing woman had sent me no pneumatique. She projected instead, in the moment of her reproach, the temperament of tardy friends in the present age of obscenely prolific cellphones, wherein there is a constant confounding of self-ish whim for contingency. I suspect one can know the backphrasers of the world even amidst those who do not sing. They are those who think they pay a courtesy, having made an appointment, by updating one by cellphone text on the progress of their tardy arrival—permitting the completion of their journey to be a moveable feast, elevating the value of *their* time to that of a Saint. They believe that sending updates during their untimely voy-age is akin to timeliness, and they resent it if their messages receive no reply. This is accompanied, as well, with intimations that the party that has kept the appointment suffers from an angry rigidity that can be traced to causes outside of the incident. And when they do appear, they always ask, "How long have you been waiting?" To which I always reply, "The difference between your time of arrival and our appointment."

Again, "You're waiting for me," she had said. To whom, if anyone, I wondered, did she wish to remain in synchronization, in parallel time? I thought of how, when a passenger train is nearly empty, I enjoy walking down the center aisle of the interior of the coaches, in the opposite direction of the train's path, especially when it is leaving a station, or passing a platform at slow speed. And I take pleasure in seeking to keep parallel to me some person on the platform of the depot: to give the illusion to myself that I am stationary, like that person on the platform, in relation to the train. A pianist in a backphrasing instant is as the moving train in the scenario I describe here. The walker in the aisle is the backphrasing singer. Who does the backphrasing singer look to on the figurative platform for reference, as she sings straight out from the stage, in perpendicular relation to my line of sight as pianist, and seemingly, too, in perpendicular focus to the course of the musical train?

In other words: Is there someone in the audience with whom she wishes to remain parallel, or does she wish to remain parallel with the entire stationary audience as the music moves on? She can backphrase by walking toward the last car of the musical train, but she cannot walk past the last car without disaster. She must at last move back to her place, lest the conductor who leaves the little cardboard slip on the back of her seat ask for another fare. But she might be so intent on keeping the beloved figure on the platform parallel to her frame of reference that she will almost walk out of the back door of the last car of the train, or seem to resent the train moving past the platform. She might pull the brake cord—yet do so without stopping the train—so that she might hope to float behind like a glimmering balloon tied to the last car's back railing, like a candidate conducting a train campaign of stump speaking without stopping at the towns. The indulgent backphrasing singer walks as on a treadmill with a belt of finite length, staring long at the figure on the platform— thinking she can walk the aisle of the train and keep parallel to her beloved even after the train is out of the station, like a smitten athlete staring at her trainer, as the latter stands on the gym floor next to her treadmill.

I think of all the parting romantic couples I have seen in this scenario, united and then ultimately split by the length of a platform. The backphrasing singer: she, as well, ultimately teases to the audience a motion, a trip, which the audience cannot long share. The backphrasing singer hints at the seeming generosity and love I have seen affected by many theater performers for their public on the figurative platform—performers who, to me, broadcast a sort of hostile charity, a pretense to a universal affection that translates: You wish you were doing this, too, but cannot. The condescension extends to the backphrasing singer giving the impression she thinks herself responsible for eliminating the Doppler Effect for the beloved on the figurative platform left behind by the passing train. Does she not thus create an intonation problem in time, as a penalty for her condescension to assist the stationary?

And yet, again, if a pianist—the classically trained pianist—senses, hears, the romance between the stationary figure on the platform and the backphrasing singer moving down the coach aisle, a matchmaker's courtesy kicks in, and he slows down to give the lovers more time to line up, to lock gazes. But this denies the backphrasing singer her vain, her dramatic effect. She does not wish really for more time at the platform. Hence, again, the scornful utterance to the piano-train, "You're waiting for me!"

Or perhaps the backphrasing singer sees herself as a figure on the depot platform. She agreed to take the train trip with me. She agreed to the time for meeting at the station. The train, say, was to come at 3:00 PM. I went to the station, yet even at 2:59:59 the singer was not on the platform. Though the trip was planned as mutual, the singer did not want me to remain at the station. She wished me to board the train and for her alone to play at the missed train scene. But this is, of course, an affectation. She is not late. All latecomers—almost without exception—have timed their lateness down to an eighth note's breadth. The timely person who was on time for the train is in fact less timely in respect to precise intersection in time. The timely languish in wasted buffers, and then suffer the collective, rigid, average tempo of the train. The backphrasing singer then has the pleasure of her affected individual spotlight. But it is she who becomes wasteful, heedless in respect to energy— for to keep parallel with the train she must take a cab to the next station with such precision so as to be sure to miss the train again, and to repeat the ritual at each station's platform. But this, too, is by plan. The pianist remains precise as to rate in theater music; the singer is precise as to intermittent intersection. But, again, any attempt from the pianist to facilitate the intersection is an unwelcome courtesy.

As I sat on the bench in the seconds after she said, "You're waiting for me," and considered the thoughts I express above, I wondered: Is a train with no passengers the ideal? When I have been out late running and I have seen westbound trains on Long Island pass by on the lonelier branches, they have appeared almost unmanned and passengerless, a player piano on the rails.

When a train leaves a station, is the slight jolt, the restoration of tautness between the cars, the reminder of this ideal—that the rubato is to be very limited if there is to be a train?

However, it started to seem to me that the musical results of her backphrasing, and all the other implications from it that I cite above, might lead to an unrealized ideal if it emanated from a single consciousness. No rudeness, no selfishness, would be implied by any of the above if all the effects were realized and experienced from a mind of one. I recalled Mozart's articulation of the ideal for a single consciousness at the piano:

"That I always remain strictly in time surprises everyone. They cannot understand that the left hand should not in the least be concerned in a *tempo rubato*. When they play, the left hand always follows." I had become a *they* of two left hands to the figurative right hand of my backphrasing singer.

Mozart implies that his left hand is a strict accompanist in steady time—as is the expectation for the whole pianist in musical theater. But Mozart leaves his right hand to handle the rubato, to handle his notion of backphrasing. Yet even to this day, almost every pianist one will hear, when they engage in rubato of any kind, has both hands locked together. I have heard some pianists affect, by coordination *between* the hands, the intellectual independence called for by Mozart, but, again, I suspect their result is achieved by carefully rehearsed manual choreography.

Could Mozart himself do what he suggests? If so it would be as wondrous a feat of mind as Melville imputes to the Sperm Whale in *Moby Dick*, due to the immense mass isolating the two eyes of that animal: "True, both his eyes, in themselves, must simultaneously act; but is his brain so much more comprehensive, combining, and subtle than man's, that he can at the same moment of time attentively examine two distinct prospects, one on one side of him, and the other in an exactly opposite direction? If he can, then is it as marvellous a thing in him, as if a man were able simultaneously to go through the demonstrations of two distinct problems in Euclid."

I submit that one imagine—if a single pianist were in their left hand to be as steady in tempo as Mozart's ideal implies, and as steady in his left hand as the musical theater ideal demands of both his hands; yet as free in his right hand as the Mozart ideal implies, and as free in his right hand as the backphrasing theater singer is in her musical role—that the miracle of such independence would be as a single runner straddling two adjacent treadmills, both machines running at slightly different speeds in the same direction, yet the runner able to maintain stability as if on a single machine's band.

One could become, if able to realize Mozart's standard, as both the selfish friend giving cellphone updates as to their arrival time *and*, at the same time, be the other who has strictly kept the appointment and is waiting in place. One could text the other part of themselves and say: "You, left hand, stay put, but I will arrive when I see fit because I can tell you about my approach intermittently." In that Cosmos of solitary mind a sense of ensemble requires that only one party be timely for both to be timely.

But when a classical pianist—both his hands yoked in rubato, as if he had two right hands by Mozart's standard—plays as a classical pianist for a theater singer (she as another right hand by Mozart's standard), it is as a comedy and chaos of three right hands. Three right hands cannot clasp. There must be a left hand and its duty somewhere. Thus, the woman before me, in saying, "You're waiting for me," was perhaps saying the equivalent of "Let us shoot for a great master's unreachable ideal of consciousness, though it may take two to realize it."

Until the single consciousness can reach that

standard, let me sing in praise of the warning, "You're waiting for me."

Again, in common practice classical playing (as for art songs), the pianist and voice are yoked together, perfectly, as to rhythm and tempo: two ships moving against the same shore of audience at the same rate! This form of performance art seems to teach a fear of a Cosmos that has no ultimate Newtonian synchronization. It compels one to move in such perfect tandem so as to avoid any Relativistic outcomes as per Mr. Einstein's laws. It lives in fear of ending on a different clock than the partner's, such that *allargando* and *accelerando* are kept perfectly matched between the two; so that even if Relativistic effects are symbolically invoked or risked, from the point of view of an audience member in a different frame of reference, the two performing travelers have the same reading on *their* clocks from beginning to end.

But the backphrasing singer of theater and popular music plays as if with Relativistic factors, risks, and outcomes, independent of her fellow performer. In order for the backphrasing singer to land behind the accompanist in evident sound for her listeners, she has already pre-heard the landing of the strict beat that has yet to fall. She has rushed ahead in mind at near the Cosmic speed limit so as to be *heard* to sing more slowly to others, to those listening in a different frame of reference. Yet after the backphrasing risk is taken, theater singers realign with the steady accompaniment partner once more—in a miraculous silent leap and calculation. They realign themselves to the pianist's present without consequence.

Her voice remains behind while backphrasing but perhaps her body—or some part of her being—remains always parallel to the accompaniment, allowing her to stay attached to a Newtonian constant, an omnipresent. The backphraser reminds one, by a portent embedded in a yoyo means of art, of a fear that future space travel suggests. The backphraser may stand for this: With the coming of the railroad came the uniformity of railroad time. But with the coming of Einsteinian Relativity came the intimation that there can be no such thing—no railroad time, and thus no future starship time between the planet depots of the Cosmos. We live in fear that a twentieth-century scientific revelation will at last throw us back to an unscientific time of localized timetables. Does the backphraser represent the hope that train time will not be lost in a Relativistic future of space travel, and that a cure can be found? Is the backphraser, is she the ultimate hero, hinting that one day a single inertial frame of reference will be found for all? Perhaps even greater than her self-faith that she can take liberties because of her equal power to amend, is her faith that a Universal frame of reference will ultimately be found if she has the power to return to it.

The backphraser suggests a future power that she can steal (can play rubato with our space travel) and then give back without the Cosmos noticing, or ever accusing her of stealing even when she engages in rubato in plain sight? Perhaps backphrasing intimates the greater Romantic synchronicity (over Einstein's seemingly immutable insight), the Newtonian hope that permits the James Kirk of *Star Trek* or the Han Solo of *Star Wars* to play their rescues yet return home to the same era they left, without having to wind forward even a bit their watches, or to need hear of the success of their missions only from the descendants of those whom they rescued.

The backphrasing singer wishes her time travel— her speed changes, her individualized rubato—at last to be only spatial change. She wishes to risk the perception of the Relativistic without returning home to find her loved ones long dead and gone. She wishes to risk rubato and warped time and great speeds yet land in the green room with her public and pianist still parallel to her frame of reference, though they sat still and steady through the concert.

Is the theater singer's stage fright a residual fear of possible Relativistic consequences, that one night she might backphrase so far after her steady accompanist that she might return to Earth after the piece's end, after the double bar, and find herself too alone, she looking at an empty stage and empty house under ghost light? But if she is careful she remains the beacon of the ice clock of humanity's undefeated Newtonian dream.

The concert came that night after the rehearsal, and when the same passage presented itself I did not wait for her. Then this woman, practitioner in a field in which the suitable uniform is a thigh-hugging, sequin dress, sacrificed herself in display of an unrecognized high-mindedness. And as I kept rigid time and let her fly about the Cosmos, the fabric around her moving thighs seemed as a chainmail made of fireflies.

I looked past my pit lamp to those glimmers and was reminded of the times, as a runner, I have paused in the night forest to watch the insect lightning—their flashes giving one God's perspective on the brevity of stellar lives. Then I flew off as an owl, my feathers restored, amidst familiar faces at the stage door.

Practice Rooms: From the Windows of Diligence

S tarting in tenth grade I rode my bicycle to school so that I could start practicing in the concert grand piano practice room by 6:45 AM each morning. A custodian left the door and the piano's fallboard unlocked for me. I do not remember ever seeing this custodian, but the room was always open at the appointed time, and I always locked it behind me when I left for my first class. Was it because another student saw the custodian make his rounds, or was it because the room at that time had no window, that a friend told me during eleventh grade math class that a virtuosic custodian practiced in that room every morning? I told my classmate that it was I whom he had heard, but he was not convinced. I felt driven to be known as the source of the legend. Now I do not know why I did not think it then more gratifying to foster the myth. I hid in that practice room yet still wished to be known as the person behind the covering door.

I went into that room to win the attention of female classmates. Yet at the same time I had such a specific sense of self-mythology and strictly sequential romantic rules that would lead only to *the one,* that I was always pushing ahead against full brakes no matter how powerful my Darwinistic peacock feathers became. But soon another level of complexity entered into my mind. Though I had entered the room with unremitting discipline so as to win attention from girls, I started to reach a level at which I glimpsed applications that could be made to a still higher level—applications that were above sexual spoils and thus demanding care in use of the skills I would gain in order to meet those applications. I felt I was gaining a power that could be misused.

The above ideas are the only way I can account for the little tale that follows. I went into this room one afternoon to practice. After some time had passed, I sensed someone was sitting and leaning against the outside base of the usually secured half of the large double door. The inside of the door was close enough that I could rest my back there if I pulled the bench away from the keyboard just a bit. And I could hear the dry and quiet wisp of someone's light clothes—as this unknown figure shifted—hissing on the other side. I left the room after a time to use the water fountain—or imagined that was why I left—and saw a slender, pretty, girl with long brown hair. She affected a touch of hippy look though this was 1988. I believe she asked me something. What did she say? I cannot now recall, although I knew the intention of all that was said. Did she ask, too, what I had been practicing? It had been, I think, either the first or second movements of Rachmaninoff's Second Piano Concerto—an unpardonable cliché of fostering peacock feathers in the laboratory.

But I do remember that she held a single rose. I traveled to the water fountain and back. She was still there when I returned. Did we say more as I went back into the room? I cannot recall. All the while, however, I affected that ignorance that my self-mythology demanded, though then before me was a case of both the raw goal *and* a possible starting point for the elevated romantic myth of *one* story. But since my self-mythology demanded that the story be one story, I could not start any of them lest they be the wrong start. I could hear that she remained there for a time after I went back into the room.

Later, a knock came at the door, and a friend looked in on me—a friend who did not expect to find a custodian. He asked after the rose that lay at the base of my door. Worse than when I later departed the room for the day and left the rose there outside on the school's floor was in the answer I gave to this fellow, and took my code to a monstrous level of foolish discipline and said I did not know why the flower was there. Or did he show it to me, and I threw it away, knowing all that I knew? Who was she, and where is she now? There was a case when I could have picked up an arrowhead and known the hunter-maiden who had drawn the bowstring. The room and its piano are still in the same place today, but a window has been added to the door.

In graduate school I found the common conservatory and university feature of a window on every practice room door. Some players would cover the glass with a piece of paper or a dark and opaque page from a magazine. Was this mainly done in the rooms where the pianos faced the window? I do not think so. Sometimes I even saw music stands raised and then made to lean against the doors' windows—the music rack of the stand pressed flush against the glass. These music stands were almost always empty of printed music, but I often noted to myself the embossed metal lettering that one could read through the window on the face of the stand: *Manhasset*—as if to block the view the implied opacity of an entire town from my native Long Island had been employed. I do not believe that I ever applied anything to the glass myself. The glass does not compromise the barrier for me.

I recall a time I played for singers in the atrium of a large performing arts center. This was a small presentation meant to divert patrons before they entered the main hall. The piano I played was inches away from an enormous window that flows down to the floor and the ground outdoors. Many of the patrons were elderly, and most made their way directly past the window on their way to the facility's main entrance, but one ungainly man approached the window adjacent to the lower register of the keyboard. He came very close to the glass—I like an ape or tiger or shark, and he like a child in a modern zoo or aquarium about to pat the glass. He did not. But he surprised me in how close he approached. He beckoned to a woman behind him. Perhaps he looked in and could not see me, as often happens when one looks into car or store windows and sees only a reflection? But I felt that he could see me, and I think it was because he could not hear me that he got so close.

Yet I recall times when glass and a door were not necessary to give observers a false impression of cover. For years I have noted the misconception some have as to the degree of external awareness a pianist experiences when playing casually. At parties I have worked, people stand close—even at my shoulder—and make hushed remarks as if I cannot hear them. Another's silence or quiet is not camouflage to one who is playing casually; only the full engagement of one who is playing renders another undetectable.

But even in an empty practice room one does not always find immediate solitude. One must often contend with the record of one's predecessors: perfume; body odor; the scent of food;

greasy finger prints on the keyboard; excessive choices of heat or cold (some adjacent rooms share a thermostat); in days past, cigarette stains on the keys (those discolorations like the ends of dogwood flowers that have faded and fallen in the spring); and the use of such rooms for personal storage or assignations. Mercifully, one cannot find their predecessor's sounds left behind; a practice room user never has cause to pick up another's brass, in the firing range respect, or chance to borrow another's brass (*aes alienum*) and to form a debt.

The preceding things are offensive beyond their usual degree of transgression, because at its best, a practice room is one of the only spaces in abundance of its kind: meant to be free of all amenities, and meant to possess less signs of convenience and personality than even a modern prisoner's chamber—yet both lined up in very similar cellblocks. Some small practice rooms do not have a piano of any kind, and I have noted some of these spare spaces when they have lacked even a chair and a music stand. They call for the instrumentalist who has internalized his music. This player does not use the room as a reading room for a new piece but stands within it (I picture a violinist at this moment), solely so as to be unheard by others and to keep others unheard. I always recall the principal pleasure of having a piece by memory was to enter the room of no amenities (save that it have a piano) and to bring nothing else with me—like the survivalist who can be dropped into a wilderness area with only a knife or flint (or perhaps without even those advantages). I recall in such practice sessions the impulse to tidy the room before starting, to place any stray music stands squarely in a corner, out of sight if possible, closing the fallboard and lid of any second piano—*and* closing the lid of the piano I was using: as if, after withdrawing from everything outside of the room, one also cuts off as much as possible from within the room. I recall on occasion taking the further step of turning out the room's lights. A visual artist cannot do that. In fact, most artists always seek a studio with the best possible light from without. They cannot insulate and isolate their room without fear of blocking an external resource to their work. A practice room can boast how much sound it can exclude from outside without any fear of harming the sound it admits from within.

Perhaps the above suggests why I hold suspect those who practice in romanticized spaces or outdoors, for they seek settings full of subtle amenities. I recall a neighbor, a flautist, who practiced in her driveway: practicing meant as a kind of performance (an SOS cry of identity) and thus fraudulent as practice. This is akin to the countless guitarists who practice in parks and the ostensible authors who must write in coffee houses on laptops. They solicit the limitations of bidden attentions. This can lead at times to unusual consequences outside of finding admirers or a date. I recall, in the late twentieth-century, a good friend in graduate school who decided once to practice upon his unplugged Steinberger guitar while sitting at the edge of a fountain outside of his apartment building. He was soon surrounded by police cars, for a neighbor had reported a man with a gun.

But the hallway just outside of each practice room in a traditional university or conservatory—and the orbital walk one must make of that circuit in search of an empty room when one has used up one's assigned practice times—can yield remarkable observations and reminders in the moments before one incarcerates oneself. Yet at the same time one must often grapple with a chain of petty irritations during that walk. One can encounter empty but brightly lighted rooms that appear claimed for great periods of time: marked by a door propped open, or with an instrument left delicately idle and waiting, or a jacket on a bench or chair; or in a pianist's case, a score left on the piano's music rack. And while making one's circuit, one sometimes encounters one's rightful successor by sign-up time standing in the open doorway of the room from which one has just been evicted, they transfixed in a chat, making one wonder if the successor values his practice time. And it is often the same person who stands in the doorways outside of assigned practice times and makes one wonder if they value anyone's time at all. The dispossessed are left to circulate hyena-like if they do not have the courage to challenge, and often the dispossessed takes to an undesirable room only to be told soon—after a period of inconvenience and not rest—that their original room is open yet again. To combat this problem, one, over time, can turn to being a sort of bully based on projected ambition—by claiming a room so much in the unassigned hours that one gains a sort of implied control over it even in the scheduled times. I have done this myself. And, as well, I have used this method in fitness clubs in the treadmill section during times of marathon training.

But one can hear marvelous things when making repeated circuits of the practice room hallways. One can hear a piece rendered as if sundered, the temporal gaps between one's orbital passes near a noted room imposing rips into a piece being played without pause. Of course the sundering does not rip adjacent passages and leave the latter section to be resumed on one's next pass in orbit; a loss is noted. But of course, though this is rare, the walker in orbit—provided the player the walker tracks is conducting repetition in an exquisitely yet fortuitously timed way—can sometimes hear the sundered piece as if with no gaps, as if it has floated in a moving pause until the orbiter has returned for another pass. I have also heard by virtue of orbit, pieces—because more than one person is practicing the same piece at the same time—pieces that seem to run backward, in respect to adjacent passages, chance seeming to transcribe a work as if into Beethoven's sketchbooks, or rendering them like a wagon wheel or hubcap viewed from the side at a very precise speed. And how many times have I orbited the circuit and heard two seemingly parallel, almost synchronized, performances of the same piece, only to find at last that the players had been paralleling two different utterances of the same exposition (first time vs. second time); or paralleling the first section of an exposition with the first part of a recapitulation? Perfect pairings are suddenly revealed to be May/December romances. This false synchronization also resembles moments afforded on some very twisting suburban mountain bike courses, when the looping closeness of differing sections of a single trail often gives one the impression that another rider is nearly adjacent and parallel to one's own exact place on the course, when in fact they may be very far ahead or behind on the same path (and moving perhaps in the opposite direction though appearing to do otherwise for a falsely parallel instant).

If the player or players are aware of the orbiter in the hallway, they may adjust—even unconsciously—to show their best selves to this passing moon. I have walked as a moon over this circuit many a time. If one is known to be making the orbit, one can affect the tides of the practice room players in many ways. One can influence a player's wobble and enforce a stable planetary rotation. One can cause an eclipse and influence a player to cease practicing while one passes. One making the rounds, the orbit, is also like the guard in a prison film. If the players react, they know he is present. When they react, they are not focused on their work, but are as inmates in an escape plot. They are not penitent, but performing and feigning sleep, and then returning, after the guard passes, to plans of their breakout recital. One making this orbit is also like a runner on a circuit in a forest, disturbing a finite amount of deer in a finite amount of preserve. Yet the smartest practicers are like the smartest deer: they react only so as to change positions to a site where they will not have to react.

But when I have felt undetected in my search for a room, I have wondered why, as well, that a room that is silent but occupied—by a pianist sitting motionless and quiet on the bench—is the most interesting of rooms. That pianist perchance may not be resting, but may have surpassed all amenities, even his instrument. This effect is augmented when seen in relation to modular practice rooms. They are as chambers within chambers.

The doubly insular quality of such rooms suggests that the player lives in an instrument case and is himself as much the protected element of the case as the instrument. From afar, modular practice rooms look as if they are about to be carried away by a giant hand, that hand Lord of all that occurs within. One is the encased axe of God in such a room. But I have encountered modular practice rooms in only one institution.

At last, into my favorite practice room in graduate school I would go: a room much like the one in high school, for it had a concert grand piano. For a period of time after entering, I myself would have to resist the urge to adjust the nature of my practicing based upon the identities of those whom I suspected to be in orbit in the hallway outside. Or sometimes, in the late hours of a practice room night, I might pause and listen to hear who was still about in the other rooms by the sound of their own practicing. I would suddenly hear another's playing, even at a distance—like the muffled report of gunfire from the opposite, far, end of a shared but vast shooting range. The individual stations at a range are much like practice rooms. The open area beyond the isolated stations, where the targets hang, are usually not separated—just as in the practice rooms the vibrating medium of the air into which sound travels cannot be, at last, separated fully. It would be a violation of etiquette to shoot at another man's target, so in due time I would also endeavor to check that my practicing was not a mere attempt to impress a stranger at the far end of the hallway (by playing a passage with greater ease myself that I could hear was trouble to him). It was then that *I* was as a mere prisoner in a cell, attempting to pass a threatening note to an inmate—about what I would do when at last on the outside, as if the most important work of all was in a recital and not in that solitary remove. Thus I returned to my own earnest playing and blocked out the sound of all others. But just before this full commitment, I have sometimes held down the keys silently or the damper pedal in order to hold onto a boisterous voice in the hallway or a cheerful visitor's voice that has just departed the room.

What is the aim of a practice room? It would seem—especially in a university or conservatory, where there are so many such rooms—to supply a space so that my neighbor, in his room, does not hear me, and so that I, in mine, do not hear him. And yet even in the most modern facilities one almost always hears one's neighbor—even at a considerable distance—to some degree. So what, at last, is the final barrier that shuts out the sound of one's neighbor? One's own sound, the sound of one's own playing. One's own sound is the final and most secure wall.

And I submit that the creation of such a barrier is the principal function of one's own focused playing in the practice room. But if its principal function is to be as a wall—something holding other things out; as an insulation rather than as the prized and cultivated interior object; as the shell rather than the pearl; as the cover rather than the text—then *what* is the innermost and prized thing in the practice room if it is not the reuttered thoughts of another, those reuttered thoughts maniacally repeated as if to meet some aim of ultimate polish? If the sound of one's own extremely focused playing is but the sound of some false stone polisher, then what are the stones, what are the gems that rest within the protection of the wall one erects, those gems shining and polished already without contact and refurbishing? One's own Unbidden thoughts!

In the practice room the Unbidden comes because I am so agent in my senses during engagement in a private task, that such agency leads to a still better passive action and receptivity of the Mind, a better receptivity than achieved by the principal action of the practicing. The most engaged practicer knows his best efforts are but a fortress into which he climbs rather than as a gallery wall to be beheld from without. The best things are what steal into my mind, entirely unrelated to the piece. I would hear the Unbidden and not principally, if at all, the sounds of the composer.

No use of headphones or soundproof room will achieve the like effect. The wall of sound made by one's self in the practice room is different. With such playing it is a full engagement of the mechanism of self that then permits the admittance of the Unbidden. So it is not ultimately, then, the mere sound that blocks. Such practicing engages so much will that the intuitive portals are then most widened. One practices until the Unbidden ideas are free to enter the otherwise too full inner space of self. One must, in the practice room, crowd out the earthly and then admit the population boom that can always find more room in the finite space of agent Mind—like the ever-increasing but never accruing population of souls in Heaven. The Unbidden can only slip in when there is not a single remaining place on the guest list.

The nature of this wall of sound makes me think of a yard's back corner where all the dogs and cats of my life are buried. The sandy Long Island soil there must be reinforced by the skeletons. The fully engaged practicer creates a wall around himself and in his own senses as if with an air-soil made dense with the rib cages of dead sonatas. The pianist building the wall that admits the Unbidden uses these skeletons, these rib cages of form, the once agent thoughts of composers reduced to expositions and recapitulations, as an eagle feathering its rigid eyrie with castoff things.

To be so engaged in good practicing that only the Unbidden can at last find room and place! The best of the Unbidden comes when the most force has been applied as if to keep it out. That conundrum has been the great blessing yet task of practicing the piano for me.

The practicer who courts the Unbidden with his sound—that sound is best when it blocks out all other influence, including the most stray observations of the practicer. But that sound is also best if it is unheard outside the practice room, when it cannot be heard by another, when it does not try to reform another, when only the self is reformed.

By the time of that graduate school practicing I was almost altogether past playing for reasons that had sent me at first into practice rooms (for the girls), and yet past, too, rehearsing for the high cause I had later discovered in the high school practice room (playing in service of music above sexual gain). I entered then into the practice room as the player with no moons, as the one truly solitary, the one using the penitentiary for penitence, the one whose barrier of sound makes his mind receptive to the arrival of Unbidden ideas from within.

But the practice room's best effect rarely carries itself to the platform of the recital hall. The malaise one feels in moving into a performance space is perhaps far more significant than a case of nerves. The pianist there can find the disconcerting, even dis-*concerting*, effect of echo. Hearing one's own echo is as wading downstream in a creek and seeing one's own stirred silt return and pass one's own steps. In hearing one's own echo one recovers the common passive reception of external sound even while engaging in a fully active role. One cannot block one's own sound while playing in a recital hall. In the recital hall, the wall one can construct in the practice room in the name of the Unbidden can come crashing down on the builder. The sound of one's own wall comes back and compromises the totality of the wall. One is only secure behind one's wall if one does not sense its outer side, the listener's side, the listener's side in respect to idle passivity. We play in recital as if to keep ahead and outside of our own reverberation, to keep ahead of hearing the same thing that a large and critical public hears from afar. We work hopelessly in recital against the compromise of the awareness of the many—that numbered *many* always more narrow in consciousness than the infinitude of the one who is fully engaged. The solitary consciousness that labors such that the Unbidden can be admitted always admits more than the mere inspirations caused by witnesses. Those mere inspirations are what account for the truest form of stage fright.

I find that in the recital space of greater life, what with my Puritan conscience, that my efforts subject me to a long echo. Is that the reason I prefer practice rooms over recital halls? Because there one's actions do not reverberate for self-examination? The practice room allows one to be hyper self-critical in the present, but the object of criticism, the sound, the ghost in the conscience, disappears almost at once. I know men whose consciences live naturally as if in practice rooms; mine is in a vast hall.

But into what space does the player have to contract so that he does not have to hear himself? Again: the practice room. Eventually the smartest pianist will close himself off from his own sound and refrain from exporting to the platforms of the world the renderings, the buffering walls, he perfects by repetition in that inner chamber of the practice room. And instead he will only export what he heard in the innermost chamber of mind, there closed off from the sound of other instruments, and, at last, from even his own sound. One never uses headphones in the practice room to block out outer influence, but one uses effort and thereby discovers headphones that attach to one's within. In the practice room the march is upstream, always, and one never wades in one's own silt.

Before I had the discipline to transcribe into a Journal the ideas that arrived when the Unbidden joined me in the practice room, I transferred that then inapplicable elation to the next nearest form of full engagement (second to practicing) that I could find. I became a runner. Not long ago I ran in a forest that I frequent: Makamah Preserve, on the outskirts of Northport Village on Long Island. It is a woods with a little over one hundred acres and with a white-blazed loop trail over undulating and hilly terrain. On the day I cite here, I kept my resolve to repeat the loop, even when I reached the trail head and felt a lazy impulse to leave the woods. I recall reinforcing my resolution with a thought: Many instrumentalists decide to pass over a repeat sign, that sign and its section observed all of the time in preparation but suddenly ignored in performance due to external influence. This run was, up until then, far more like an uninspired hour in the practice room than on the stage, so I could not award myself too much credit in my decision to observe the repeat. But I was to be rewarded for my faith to an extended form—and my resolve to ignore what can seduce one too early out of that figurative practice room of the woods: rest, water, and the false sense of self-assurance that what little one has already done is enough.

During this second loop I worked very hard and lost awareness of my surroundings. As I ascended a considerable hill before the trail makes a critical intersection with an ancient and unpaved road—all this amidst a maturing cathedral of second growth oaks—I noted suddenly a brilliant and hale red fox, red as a new crayon seen obliquely, he running parallel to and as if with me, no more than five to ten yards on my right. Somehow we both had not heard the other, and we were both mutually surprised and unmoved from our respective parallel courses for a few glorious seconds. The fox accelerated. He was an ossia in red to my beaten path on the trail.

The fox looked to be in fine condition, and I was close enough to see that his coat seemed powdered with dust. I was so overjoyed at the sight of him that I believe I laughed, or spoke some involuntary words. When I reached the crest of the hill and the intersection, he vanished into the trackless woods beyond. I hoped to see him again, but I did not. Yet I may have heard him as he went bushwhacking into the southwest. The fox had been jolted as I have been by knocks at the practice room door. Sometimes one continues to play and affects not hearing—affects failing to hear a knock at the door—but that can last only so long.

I have wondered what permitted both parties to approach the other so closely without warning. I have speculated that, to a degree, the fox may have heard me approach, but either did not identify me as a large threat (for do not even the squirrels and chipmunks make a great crash in the leaf litter?) or, perhaps, he had identified me and was willing to cling for as long as possible to some investment I could not detect: a pursuit of game, or following a path of travel that for him represented some sort of efficiency or safety that I could not assess.

But, ultimately, I think he did not hear me, as one working hardest in a practice room does not hear. Though I recall almost no ambient and covering noise—no music of wind or weather or birds—I believe the fox was gifted for the moment with the deafness granted by full engagement, as was I.

As in so many cases, is it not because we do

not hear the approach of another that we are able to get so close—and yet so close to something so much better than that other? We live at times in the practice rooms of our skulls, and in our most engaged moments we are graced by the approach of the Unbidden fox. Or we are as blessèd as the fox. How much closer an audience could get to me if they could not hear me, perhaps as close as when I cannot hear them. Upon what else has the sound of the piano permitted me to sneak—or allowed to sneak up on me: as fox and man in parallel? In working with full engagement in practice rooms for so long in my life, is the best I can say for those many hours that they often allowed me to sneak up on myself?

I left the white-blazed trail, just for a little while, after I reached its intersection with the old and sandy road. I was so distracted by my elation from the Unbidden fox that I needed to pause. I followed the old woods road to the wondrous and familiar ruin of a house foundation, a sunken dereliction amidst the trees. I do not think it supported a very large house when the land that is now the surrounding forest was a clear pasture, but I believe the house could have sheltered a piano. I have found no evidence to support my suspicion, yet in the springtime, during runs of only mild intention, I never fail to note the myrtle flowers that bloom in a wide circle about the foundation, in greatest concentration below the former position of a door.

About the Author

Jack Kohl is a pianist and author living in the greater New York City area. He is the author of THE PAUKTAUG TRILOGY: *That Iron String, Loco-Motive,* and *You, Knighted States,* and *Bone Over Ivory,* a collection of essays.